CRIME & CULPABILITY

A JANE AUSTEN MYSTERY ANTHOLOGY

REGINA JEFFERS   RIANA EVERLY   JEANETTE WATTS
ELIZABETH GILLILAND   MICHAEL RANDS
EMMA DALGETY   LINNE ELIZABETH

EDITED BY
ELIZABETH GILLILAND RANDS

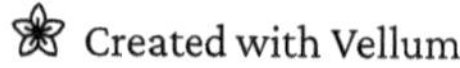 Created with Vellum

FOREWORD

BY REGINA JEFFERS

Although publishers long ago labeled Jane Austen-inspired pieces as "niche" literature, they erred. Austen's touch can be found in a variety of genres: women's literature, romance, variations, historical fiction, paranormal, fantasy, and mystery. Over the years, I have written several cozy mysteries using Austen's characters. It is easy to concoct a mystery story around her plots, for Miss Austen provides us with a variety of starting points.

For example, without good reason, General Tilney sends Catherine Morland from Northanger Abbey. He has no care for her safety upon the road alone. Meanwhile, his eldest son seduces Isabella Thorpe and then abandons her. In *Pride and Prejudice*, Mr. Wickham produces a multitude of lies that mislead Elizabeth Bennet and others in Meryton. He seduces innocents. He plots with Mrs. Younge. Frank Churchill, in *Emma*, pursues one woman while claiming a secret betrothal with another. Mr. Willoughby leads Marianne on in *Sense and Sensibility*. He abandons his pregnant mistress. Both actions occur because he must marry for money. Henry Crawford blatantly flirts with an engaged woman and then elopes with her. Tom Bertram is responsible for many of the major plot points that dominate the start of *Mansfield Park*. His gambling debts are part of the reason why his father, Sir Thomas, must go to Antigua to take care of his financial problems. Tom's debts also mean that Edmund will not be able to move into the Parsonage at Mansfield Park when he is ordained. Mr. Elliot abused Mrs. Smith's trust in *Persuasion* and later attempts to claim Anne to wife so he might prevent Sir Walter from remarrying and producing an heir to replace him. Austen offers her readers a "secret," perhaps not a major crime, but one that can be employed by a skilled contemporary writer.

As "the lady" was the precursor of the modern romance, Austen also added to the mystery genre. The mystery/suspense plot requires the ending to be a restoring of order. Does not each of Austen's heroines solve a "mystery" of sorts to bring her world to order? And is it not "love" that brings those involved together again and permits them to heal?

So how does one transform an Austen story to a mystery? According to W. H. Auden in "The Guilty Vicarage" found in Harper's Magazine (from a 1948 article), a mystery/detective story requires . . . "(1) A closed society so that the possibility of an outside murderer (and hence of the society being totally innocent) is excluded; and a closely related society so that all its members are potentially suspect (*cf.* the thriller, which requires an open society in which any stranger may be a friend or enemy in disguise). Such conditions are met by: (a) the group of blood relatives (the Christmas dinner in the country house); (b) the closely knit geographical group (the old world village); (c) the occupational group (the theatrical company); (d) the group isolated by the neutral place (the Pullman car).

"In this last type the concealment-manifestation formula applies not only to the murder but also to the relations between the members of the group who first appear to be strangers to each other, but are later found to be related. (2) It must appear to be an innocent society in a state of grace, *i.e.*, a society where there is no need of the law, no contradiction between the aesthetic individual and the ethical universal, and where murder, therefore, is the unheard-of act which precipitates a crisis (for it reveals that some member has fallen and is no longer in a state of grace). The law becomes a reality and for a time all must live in its shadow, till the fallen one is identified. With his arrest, innocence is restored, and the law retires forever.The characters in a detective story should, therefore, be eccentric (aesthetically interesting individuals) and good (instinctively ethical) — good, that is, either in appearance, later shown to be false, or in reality, first concealed by an appearance of bad."

Let us check off the requirements as they relate to Austen's books: a closed society (✓); a closely related society, that of a village (✓); the appearance of an innocent society (✓); and a society where there is no need of the law (✓). Auden goes on to explain how "rituals" characterize the closed society and that the perpetrator of the "crimes" uses his knowledge of those *rituals* to take advantage of the community. Auden also suggests that the plot must include an individual of superior intelligence to solve the mystery and reset the harmony within the society. Look at Wickham in *Pride and Prejudice.* He uses his knowledge of the more lax care of innocents at seaside resorts so he might attempt to seduce Georgiana Darcy (at Ramsgate) and successfully compromise Lydia Bennet (at Brighton). It is only with Fitzwilliam Darcy's knowledge of Mr. Wickham's propensity for debauchery and the man's cohorts that the Bennets' world is restored.

~ Regina Jeffers

Resources:

Auden, W. H. "The Guilty Vicarage." 1948. *Detective Fiction: A Collection of Critical Essays.* Robin W. Winks, Editor. Woodstock Foul Play, 1980. 15-24.

INTRODUCTION

JANE AUSTEN: A WOMAN OF MYSTERY

By Elizabeth Gilliland Rands

Jane Austen novels...and mystery? At first it might seem like a strange combination, but Jane Austen mysteries are a popular subgenre of Austenesque fiction. There are so many Austen variations being published every year, every month, every *day*, that it can be difficult to keep up with trends, but Austen-themed mysteries have actually been around for some time. Stephanie Barron's Jane Austen Mysteries series may have been the pioneer series to begin this fascination, with her first novel, *Jane and the Unpleasantness at Scargrave Manor* published in 1996. P.D. James's novel, *Death Comes to Pemberley* (published in 2011, with a BBC miniseries to follow in 2013) continued the trend, with Shannon Hale's *Midnight in Austenland* (2012) following shortly thereafter. In the last few years, the Austen-themed mystery novels that have been published are too many to name in full, though some of the most known likely include Tirzah Price's Jane Austen Murder Mystery series, Katherine Cowley's Mary Bennet novels, Jessica Bull's Miss Austen Investigates series, and Claudia Gray's Mr. Darcy and Miss Tilney series. In addition, many of the authors included in this anthology have written their own Austen mystery variations, including *Death of a Clergyman* by Riana Everly, *What Happened on Box Hill* by Elizabeth Gilliland, *My Dearest Miss Fairfax* by Jeanette Watts, and *The Mysterious Death of Mr. Darcy* by Regina Jeffers.

Beyond Austen variations in novel form, Austen has been connected to mystery more broadly in pop culture. Jane Austen features as a character in the YouTube mystery series, *Edgar Allan Poe's Murder Mystery Dinner Party*, produced by Shipwrecked. *Midsomer Murders*, a British crime series, included an episode called "Death by Persuasion" in which a series of Austen-themed murders are committed (Hopkins para. 1). The Jane Austen Society of North America (JASNA) referenced the connections between Austen and mystery in its 2010 Annual General Meeting, with its theme "Jane Austen and the Abbey: Mystery, Mayhem, and Muslin in Portland." The Jane Austen Summer Program (JASP) similarly featured an Austen-themed murder mystery game during their 2021 conference. Beyond Jane Austen Fan Fiction (JAFF), the idea of Austen being somehow connected to mystery seems to have pervaded our broader cultural perspective.

The question, then, isn't *whether* Austen inspires mystery-related content, but *why*? What invites these connections to be made, in so much quantity, and in so many different ways? It might be tempting to accuse authors and creators of copycatting one another. However, I believe this misrepresents whatever is happening culturally to inspire so many Austen mystery variations, in so many different forms. I can only speak for myself, but when I proposed my dream Austen adaptation in JASNA's 2017 Graduate Essay Contest, I was completely unaware of most of the above-listed Austen mysteries, with the exception of Hale's *Midnight in Austenland* and James's *Death Comes to Pemberley*. I thought I was doing something different and unique by combining multiple characters and plotlines from various Austen novels into one mystery-themed story; it turns out I was on the cusp of a trend: the series written by Price and Gray, as well as the game produced by JASP, also feature mystery elements combined with multiple plotlines and characters from Austen's novels. The sheer amount of authors interested in pursuing this idea of combining elements of mystery with Austen's novels, at around roughly the same time, indicates a wider cultural trend, tapping into some common intuition about how well Austen's works and the mystery genre pair together.

So again, what invites these connections between the mystery genre and Austen's novels? I have some ideas. I suspect the other authors in this anthology might have their own, and that those who are reading these stories may deduce some theories, as well. Part of the motive for putting this anthology together was to begin this wider conversation–to bring together Austen-mystery writers and readers, and to invite us to investigate more closely why this has become such a widespread cultural trend. All the authors have included the best way to get in touch with them, along with their stories, if you would like to continue the conversation individually. We also welcome you to reach out on social media or to email Bayou Wolf Press at bayouwolfpress@gmail.com, with any questions or comments directed more broadly to the publishers and authors.

But first, some of my personal theories.

Lady Detectives

Austen shares one important aspect with the mystery genre: a largely female/female-identifying audience. Though Austen's male fans are many, Austen's readers are by and large women, and for good reason. Austen's protagonists are all women, and the voice of her omniscient narrator is distinctly feminine. Though Austen's novels can delve into deeper issues, her plots and settings revolve around the domestic. Most happenings take place in or around someone's home, and the main storyline usually centers on marriage. More than one wedding usually takes place throughout the course of the novel, and the primary conflicts often stem from the heroine's interactions with her family members. When Austen was writing, novel reading was considered to be primarily a pastime for young women, although of course there were the Mr. Tilneys of the world who were not too ashamed to admit their admiration for it.

Similarly, mysteries, and murder mysteries in particular, have often targeted a heavily female audience. Many of the most famous mystery writers have also been women, including Agatha Christie, Dorothy L. Sayers, Ruth Ware, Gillian Flynn, Sue Grafton, and Patricia Highsmith, to name a few; and many of the great fictional detectives have also been women, including Miss Marple, Jessica Fletcher, Nancy Drew, Rizzoli and Isles, and Ruth Galloway. Cozy mysteries, a popular subset of the mystery novel, are written specifically to appeal to a predominantly female audience, and for good reason. As Agatha Christie once noted, the murders featured in her novels center around "quiet domestic interest" (Ius para. 1). Like Austen's novels, cozy mysteries often feature heavily domestic subplots, with heroines who bake, sew, solve small-town mysteries, become involved in romantic subplots, grapple with family issues and other domestic concerns, and even (like Austen) sometimes tackle social justice issues. Meant to stand in contrast to "more male-oriented popular fiction" (para. 3), cozy mysteries are written for an "overwhelmingly female" audience, according to literary agent Josh Getzler (qtd. in Ius para. 14). If one needs more convincing of the domestic, feminine appeal of a cozy mystery, look no further than Hallmark–yes, the cable station that produces all the Christmas movies. Hallmark now has a sister channel, Hallmark Movies & Mysteries, with content similar in nature to the homey offerings on the flagship channel, but instead featuring mysteries with amateur-detective heroines and chaste romantic subplots.

It isn't only cozy mysteries that appeal to women audiences, though. Many writers have also noted the modern phenomenon of true crime's predominantly female audience. While no one has been able to produce a definitive reason for the mass consumption of true crime by women, many theories exist, including that the genre provides a way for women to feel safe; since women are still largely the victims of homicides and domestic violence, true crime allows its female audience members to prepare themselves for the worst and thus feel less like helpless victims, waiting for danger to strike. Additionally, in a think piece for *The Guardian*, Nancy Jo Sales connects the appeal of grisly crime to the rise in popularity of online dating. Sales notes, "Women, of necessity, have become amateur detectives, often impressively adept at researching the backgrounds of their matches and potential dates" (para. 7). While Sales makes a compelling case for the need modern women feel to suss out potential future mates, Austen's writing shows us this has long been a concern for women, and that to some degree, women have always had to be detectives to determine the character of their suitor. Who is lying, who is telling the truth? Who might be deceiving others for benign reasons, and who might be obscuring the truth for nefarious purposes? With both Sales and Austen, it becomes clear that love and marriage, the domestic, and the (hopefully) happy home have always possessed high stakes. A woman's life can be ruined, or ended, by choosing the wrong partner and not reading the clues carefully enough.

Austen, Proto-Mystery Writer

Austen remains a mysterious figure herself, who died too young, and whose life has been heavily researched, yet who still remains something of an enigma. Juliette Wells suggests that many versions of Austen exist in the minds of her readers, which is perhaps why there remains so much confusion about who she was; Wells notes "this varied set of 'Austens'" creates "a figure whose writing, and to a lesser extent whose life, lends itself to distinct and ever-changing interpretations" (para. 1). Indeed, it is not only the mystery genre that has been "married" so fruitfully to Austen's work. The 2010s saw an influx of Gothic/supernatural retellings of Austen's works; more recently, Austen's novels have been paired with fantastical elements, such as dragons, witches, and werecreatures; Austen's novels have been adapted into several languages, cultures, religious backgrounds, and political leanings; and Austen herself has been written as a time traveler, a vampire, and (of course) a detective. Austen as a figure, and her works as a whole, seem to be utterly adaptable in a way that few other authors and their oeuvre can emulate.

Austen's overall adaptability, however, does not negate the particular ties to mystery that appear again and again in JAFF, adaptations, variations, academic conferences, and pop culture. Perhaps Austen's understanding of the high stakes in marriage and romance has led to a seemingly commonly held belief that if Austen were still writing today, she would be authoring detective novels. However hard to prove this claim might be, there is some merit in the fact that in her own way, Austen *was* already writing mystery novels during her lifetime. Catherine Morland, after all, was one of the first amateur detectives in literature, even if she is not named as such in the novel. With no background, no training, no skill set to speak of, Catherine nonetheless investigates a crime she believes has been committed, narrowing in on a suspect and gathering clues to support her theory. The crime she's pursuing ultimately proves to be imaginary...or is it? Colonel Tilney may not have killed his wife physically, but he certainly does seem to have squashed her spirit—another subtle warning from Austen to read the clues carefully in choosing a potential husband.

As with this example, Austen does not always spell things out for us clearly, but leaves us to connect the pieces for ourselves, and sometimes even draw our own conclusions. (Was Charlotte wrong to marry Mr. Collins? Could Mr. Crawford really have been redeemed by Fanny's love? Just how often *did* Colonel Brandon wear his flannel waistcoat, anyway?) We must discern who is sincere, who is lying, who is hiding their true feelings, and why. As Lisa Hopkins writes, Austen "consistently invite[s]...readers to construe meaning in a discriminating, alert, and nuanced way" (para. 10). The actions of Austen's characters do not always match their words; we, as the reader, must play detective along with the heroine and look beyond the surface to discover the truth of peoples' motives, all while paying close attention to the evidence provided. Mirroring the experience of reading a good mystery novel, returning to Austen's novels again often reveals the clever sleights of hand that have been performed in the narration to obscure the truth from us until the end, when everything is happily resolved. We understand, suddenly, why Knightley develops such a strong and immediate dislike for Frank Churchill, why Captain Wentworth always seems to take more of an interest in talking to Louisa when Anne is nearby, and why Mr. Wickham decides to single Lizzy out as the Bennet sister to receive his attentions. The mystery in Austen's novels is not ever *will* a happy ending be achieved, but *how* will it be achieved, and what clues have been planted along the way to lead us there.

Crime and Circumstance

This anthology, and the authors involved, hope to pay loving tribute to the many Austen-mystery connections that exist, and to continue the conversation around why these two seemingly disparate genres (Austenesque fiction and mystery) seem to go hand-in-hand so very well. As you will see as you continue reading, we have quite a range of stories, from Regency-era murders to modern-day noirs. Continue reading to find:

- In "Order and Disorder," Regina Jeffers returns to her original character, Detective Thomas Cowan, as he and Mr. Darcy investigate a murder related to familiar faces from Darcy's past.
- In "Shadows at Northanger" by Jeanette Watts, original characters move to Northanger Abbey and soon discover the home is not as idyllic as it first seems.
- In "Death at the Races" by Riana Everly (a sequel to *Pride and Prejudice* and a Mary and Alexander short story), a trip to the horse races ends in murder.

- In "The Beginning and the End," by Elizabeth Gilliland (an Austen University Mysteries short story), Professor Walter Elias discovers he is being blackmailed and turns to an unexpected source for help.
- In "New Year, New Problems" by Linné Elizabeth, a robbery takes place in a modern club setting, after Liam Darcy and Izzy Bennet have a close encounter.
- In "Detective Woodhouse and the Gallery of Forgery" by Emma Dalgety, a painting goes missing—but no fear, Emma Woodhouse is on the case!
- In "Darcy's Revenge" by Michael Rands, a modernized, noir-styled sequel to *Pride and Prejudice,* Darcy has fallen on some hard times thanks to putting his trust in an old friend.

We hope you will enjoy playing detective with our sleuths, piecing together not only the clues of the mystery, but also how these pieces fit in with Austen's original works. Some stories are direct sequels; others introduce new characters; some are variations; and some may not clearly spell out what their direct involvement with Austen and her work might be. Watch out for a few red herrings along the way, and best of luck in solving the crime before the last page. The game is afoot!

-Elizabeth Gilliland Rands
    February 2024

Elizabeth Gilliland Rands received her PhD from Louisiana State University, where she wrote her doctoral dissertation on Jane Austen adaptations. She has presented at many conferences about Austen and her work, including two JASNA AGMs and VirtualJaneCon. She is the co-founder of Bayou Wolf Press and writes fiction under the name Elizabeth Gilliland, including the Austen University Mysteries series. (And yes, one of her stories is featured in this anthology!)

Works Cited

Hopkins, Lisa. "Criminally Funny: Sarah Caudwell's Inverted Janeism." *Persuasions On-Line*, vol. 40, no. 2, Spring 2020, n.p. https://jasna.org/publications-2/persuasions-online/volume-40-no-2/hopkins/

Ius, Dawn. "Trend Report: The State of the Cozy." *The Big Thrill*, 30 Nov. 2017, https://www.thebigthrill.org/2017/11/trend-report-the-state-of-the-cozy/. Accessed 8 Feb. 2024.

Sales, Nancy Jo. "Why Do Women Love True Crime So Much? I Have a Theory." *The Guardian*, 5 Jul. 2023. https://www.theguardian.com/commentisfree/2023/jul/05/women-love-true-crime-podcasts-theory-serial-online-dating. Accessed 8 Feb. 2024.

Wells, Juliette. "Austen's Adventures in American Popular Fiction, 1996-2006." *Persuasions On-Line*, vol 30, no. 2, Spring 2020, n.p. https://jasna.org/persuasions/on-line/vol30no2/wells.html?

ORDER AND DISORDER

BY AWARD-WINNING AUTHOR REGINA JEFFERS

Order in the Crime

George Wickham breathed a sigh of relief as the gangplank was set in place. He had been waiting in the shadows for hours for just this moment. As far as he could tell, no one was any the wiser as to what occurred earlier.

Stepping from the shadows and into the drab morning light, he quickly crossed the dock, keeping his head turned ever so slightly so no one could identify him. He paused to present the waiting clerk the necessary papers. "Welcome aboard, Mr. Schultz." As Wickham climbed down the ladder to reach the waiting rowboat, which would take him to the *Leo Belgicus*, he said a private farewell to the near poverty of his life in England and dared a prayer for a better day.

It had been fortuitous indeed when Schultz had called in at the inn where George had been sipping on an ale and wondering if he should attempt to win a few coins in the card game going on at one of the tables. He was hungry and thought to purchase a meal and let a room for a few days to see what prospects might prove beneficial in this coastal town. He had tired of sleeping on the street and in abandoned buildings, as well as staying one step ahead of the watch. He should never have sold his commission, though, at the time, he thought doing so was the only means to escape both his wife and his mounting debts. George did not know which he despised more, the constant "reminders" his fellow soldiers of what he owed them or Lydia's cloying need to hear him speak of his affection for her.

With interest, he had watched Schultz, having recognized the man from their university days. Though Schultz was a Jew and a commoner, the man had easily claimed a niche of close friends, composed of many of the more "enlightened" among the upper classes, including Darcy; both George's former friend and Schultz had participated on the same rowing team at Cambridge.

With caution, he nodded to the man. "You are Schultz, correct?"

The man looked upon him as a frown marked his forehead. "Are we acquainted, sir?"

"We were at university together," George said. "I recall your being part of the rowing team."

The man still studied him. "You possess a distinct northern England accent."

George shrugged. "Hard to disguise how a man speaks." Though he had attempted it often enough. He asked cautiously, "What brings you to this part of England?"

"Work." The man shrugged. "I am off to Amsterdam tonight. Just waiting for the ship to dock properly. With the Thames lower than usual, more ships are docking at Dover, Brighton, Hull, and Norfolk. The shipping traffic is struggling to adjust. There is no reason for me to stand out in the fog and the cold."

"Makes sense," George said. Without any real desire to leave his homeland, he had never been outside of England. Never even been to Scotland or Ireland.

"And you? What brings you to Norfolk?" Shultz asked.

"Leaving my military duties soon," Wickham declared.

"Did you see much service?"

"Years," he said with a practiced sorrowful twinge in his tone. "I fear I am not fit for London ballrooms. I cannot seem to escape the stink of war." He provided Schultz a well-rehearsed shrug, as if he was embarrassed by a service he had truly never seen. "I trained to be a clergyman, you know, but I was ordered to take lives."

Schultz gestured to an empty seat. "Why do you not join me for a meal? I despise eating alone, and you sound as if you could also use an evening of conversation."

George kept the smile from forming on his lips. If nothing more, he could enjoy an actual meal this evening. Since arriving in Norfolk, he had grabbed apples and meat pies from carts when no one was looking or dug out carrots and the like from small gardens, but the opportunities were few and far between. "Such is very kind of you. I would enjoy a civil conversation and breaking bread with you."

Three hours later, Schultz was becoming mildly inebriated, and George was considering suggesting playing cards, when a man stepped into the inn. "Mr. Schultz?"

"Here," George's companion responded, and George realized he had lost his opportunity to earn a few coins.

The stranger rushed over. "The captain, sir, sends his regrets. The harbormaster says the *Lion* cannot set sail until the morning's light. He begs your pardon, sir, for the delay. Seven of the clock, sir, if it be your pleasure."

Schultz frowned. "And the current time?" he asked, looking about the room for a clock.

"Near eleven, sir." The man waited for a response, but Schultz appeared a bit dazed; therefore, George said, "Seven is acceptable. Thank you, sir."

The man rushed away, and Schultz looked to George with a bit of confusion. "It is too . . . far . . ." Schultz slurred, "to return . . . to my home . . . and back. I cannot . . . miss . . . the ship."

"Permit me to inquire of a room from the innkeeper." George stood, initially thinking of sharing the room with Schultz, but another idea hatched as he crossed the room. "Might my friend and I have another drink?"

The innkeeper eyed him suspiciously, but he, nevertheless, fetched fresh glasses and poured what passed for "brandy" at the inn.

Carrying the drinks to the table, he spoke with a bit of regret hidden in his tone. "The innkeeper claims he has no empty rooms available."

Schultz frowned deeply. "What may . . . I do?"

George shrugged. "Sit here all night, I suppose, but I fear this is the last drink we may share. I must return to my quarters." He sipped the brandy and waited for Schultz to take the bait. There were many things George Wickham did not know, but he knew rich Englishmen, even if Schultz was a rich, Jewish Englishman. All who had money preferred their comforts and did not like to be denied otherwise.

"You've quarters . . . nearby?" Schultz slurred.

"Not too close, but close enough," George shared.

Last evening, he had discovered an empty house on the outskirts of town. Small. Well tended. A vegetable garden. A fireplace and a bed, but he had not used the bed. Nor had he taken anything from the house beyond food and the firewood, so he could make himself a place before the hearth and know warmth. He had considered going through the house to steal what had value, but his father's voice in his ear had kept George's actions small, and now he was glad he had performed in a manner of which his father would have approved. "Modest, but more comfortable than a room at this inn," he murmured. What he would do if those who owned the house were within when he and Schultz reached it, George did not rightly know. He would cross that bridge when the time came.

Schultz opened his purse to fish out a couple of coins for the innkeeper, and George nearly swallowed his own tongue. The man was well let. "I will hand them to the innkeeper," he assured. He started away. "We require one more coin."

Shultz's brows drew together in doubt, but he left the purse open for George to help himself. It was very tempting to grab the purse and run, but the inn was too full of customers, all of whom who could identify him. Instead, he selected only one coin. Handing off all but the one required for a hackney, he paid the innkeeper. Returning to the table, he bent to say softly, "Permit me to fetch a hack." Schultz reached for his purse a second time, but George pushed his hand away. "My privilege. You have done enough this evening."

That had been a good quarter hour earlier. He had asked the hack to let them off at one of the most outer streets of the town so they might walk. George knew the cold air would assist in sobering up his companion, but there were several containers of homemade beer and wine available in the house's dry cellar. He'd had a cup last evening. Moreover, he did not wish the hackney driver to know of their destination.

"Not too much further," he told Schultz. "Around the bend in the road."

"Like . . . living alone?" Schultz asked.

"Letting the house. Temporarily." George explained.

"Not much . . . about," Schultz remarked.

"A coach line, not too far removed. Behind the trees yonder there be a well-worn path to the sea and the docks further along." He paused to note how the house still appeared unoccupied. His breathing eased: The pretense could continue. "Welcome," he announced with a sweeping gesture of his arm. He went ahead of Schultz and fished the key from the flower pot a second time.

"This is all . . . quite splendid . . . of you," Schultz said, as George unlocked the door and let it swing wide.

"Permit me to light a candle." George went ahead of the man. He returned immediately with the candle. "There is a bed in the next room, if you wish to rest. Trunk at the foot has extra blankets and such."

"What . . . of you?" Schultz was still having some difficulty forming his thoughts.

"I'll bed down before the fire. Quite accustomed to doing so. No great loss," George assured. "Thinking of having another beer first. To take the chill off."

"I'd not mind . . . one, if there be . . . a spare." Schultz swayed in place.

"You settle in," George instructed. "I'll fetch the beer."

So, as Schultz made his way to the small bedchamber, George claimed two mugs from the shelf. He had washed the one he had used previously and put it away the last time he was in this house. He knew where the beer could be found, as well as a small box of elixirs used to treat a variety of ailments.

"How long will . . . you be here?" Schultz called from the bedchamber. Wickham knew the cold had driven away some of the man's earlier stupor.

"Not long," George called back. "I have a promise of a change of circumstances." He dropped a half dozen drops of laudanum in the beer and a bit of clove to cover the taste. He returned to the door of the sleeping quarters. "Do you want the beer in this room or would you care to sit at the table?"

"I've an early . . . call," Schultz said. "Perhaps . . . I shouldn't have . . . more. Might you . . . wake me at . . . five?"

George knew disappointment once more. He had thought to steal the man's purse and disappear into the night. "I will see to it," he assured. "I will leave the beer on the table in case you are thirsty."

With a nod and words of gratitude, Schultz turned towards the bed. Frustrated, but not deterred, George placed a blanket and a small pillow before the hearth and laid down, but rest would not come. Schultz had enough in his purse to last George a month or more. Could the man have more on his person or the bag he had carried over his shoulder most of the evening? George could not recall whether Schultz's family were in the jewelry business or were bankers, but he instinctively knew they were rich. Very rich. And it was time they shared with the likes of him.

Disorder in the Investigation

"Mr. Cowan, sir," Mr. Thacker announced, and Darcy looked up to see the former Bow Street Runner stride into the room.

Darcy's wife was on her feet faster than he was. "Thomas! How are you?" she greeted the man, extending both hands to claim those of Cowan. "We have missed you, sir. You must plan to dine with us soon."

Cowan accepted her hands graciously. Like every man with good sense, the investigator had fallen under Elizabeth's spell.

"Your hands are cold, Thomas. Where are your gloves? It is chilly outside."

"I fear I placed them down when I am in the middle of an investigation, ma'am, and forget to retrieve them," Cowan said with a touch of embarrassment.

"Fitzwilliam, Thomas requires another pair of gloves," she stated the obvious.

Darcy extended his hand to Cowan as he nodded to his servant. "Mr. Thacker?"

"Right away, sir." The butler disappeared into the servant passage. "What brings you to Darcy House?"

"There is a reliable sighting of Mr. Wickham near Norfolk," Cowan shared. "Thought you might wish to travel with me."

Darcy looked to his wife, but there was no need. "Go. Discovering Lieutenant Wickham will not assist Lydia's reputation, but perhaps someday she might know happiness elsewhere…"

That had been more than six hours earlier. Now, as they entered an inn near the waterfront, Darcy continued to follow Cowan's lead.

"What might I fetch for you gents?" the innkeeper asked as he eyed the quality of Darcy's clothes.

"An ale for me," Cowan responded. "And you, Darcy?"

The innkeeper's eyebrow rose in obvious recognition of the Darcy name. "An ale will do," Darcy responded.

Cowan wasted no time in making his inquiries. He placed a small bag full of coins on the table. "My friend and I are looking for a man supposedly seen in the area of the docks. Likely fashions himself as a former soldier and displays a penchant for cards."

"Could be any number of fellows," the innkeeper claimed.

"But he is not 'any number' of men. He has deserted his post in the army and abandoned his wife, and cheated nearly fifty merchants out of income across more than a dozen shires. I imagine most of them would be delighted to claim this bag of coins," Cowan suggested with a lift of his brows. "As you are not so eager, I assume the man we seek did not cheat you."

The innkeeper shifted his weight several times before he shared, "Think I might'n know the man, though he does not owe me money. Found himself a fellow who paid for a meal and drinks. A golden goose. Overheard the one you seek say he had a room elsewhere they could share."

Cowan pulled out the miniature of George Wickham, which Darcy had furnished him. "This be the man for whom we search. Much younger, but still a 'pretty' man. Is this the same man of whom you spoke?"

"Yelp. That be him."

"When was the last time you saw him?" Cowan slid the bag closer to the table's edge.

"Three days ago," the innkeeper said with confidence. "The other fellow was to sail on the *Lion*, but, for some reason, it could not leave until the next morning."

Darcy knew their next stop would be speaking to the harbormaster.

"Might we have our ale?" Cowan asked. "And perhaps a stew or whatever is fresh?" With a nudge of Cowan's finger, the bag of coins fell on the floor, and the innkeeper quickly scooped it up and dropped it in his apron pocket.

"Should we not learn who was to sail on the *Lion*?" Darcy asked.

"We will, but we both require a meal. I expect it will be a very long night."

And it was exactly that. The harbormaster confirmed the *Le Lion du Nord* had but one passenger: Mr. Jacob Schultz.

"What do you know of Schultz?" Cowan asked as they walked towards the town and Darcy's waiting coach.

"How came you to believe I hold knowledge of Schultz?"

Cowan chuckled. "I imagine Mrs. Darcy reads you quite well."

Darcy ignored the comment, for the idea both pleased and frustrated him at the same time. "A Jacob Schultz attended Cambridge during the same years as I. He was on the same rowing team."

"And his family?" Cowan questioned.

"We were not close beyond the rowing team," Darcy admitted. "Though I enjoyed debating philosophy with him. If I recall correctly, Schultz's family resided in Richmond. Related to the Grose family."

"The jewelers?" Cowan questioned.

"Yes, the ones who fitted up King George's crown."

Before Cowan could respond, a rough-looking young man stepped before them and snatched the cap from his head. "Pardon, sirs. I hears you be searchin' for the fancy fellow who claims to be a sol'der."

Cowan answered for both of them. "And you know this man, how?"

"Seen him comin' out of the Molden house back nearly a week past. Followed him, cause Molden be good to me. Permits me to do chores for a meal ands sleepin' in the barn. Good people they be."

"And where are the Moldens now? Do they know the fellow from the army?"

"I don'ts think so," the man assured. "Moldens be in Herts visitin' with them's daughter. Told me so near a sennight back that they go to their girl's to meet their new grandbabe. Said I could stay in the barn at night and could have some of the turnips and such from the garden if'n I keeps an eye on the house. The army fellow stayed there two times. Once alone. Once with 'nother fellow."

Cowan placed a shilling in the man's hand. "There is another one if you direct us to the Molden house."

"Fer another, I's carry ye there meself."

A half hour later found all three of them peeking into the windows of the Molden house. "Missus Molden never be leavin' her house in such a state. It'll break her heart to sees it."

"This window on the side is open," Darcy stated. "From here, it looks as if the one on the far side, past the fireplace, might also be open."

Cowan called back. "You are correct, Darcy. This one is raised as well."

"Is there a means for us to enter the house without knocking out the window to crawl through?" Cowan asked. A deep frown marked the investigator's forehead, and Darcy knew it would not be good news.

"There be a key," Mr. Wells declared. "Army fellow finds it and gots in that way. I sees him."

"And you never went in?" Darcy asked.

"No, sirs," Mr. Wells said emphatically. "Only times I be inside be when Mrs. Molden asks me to repair a cabinet door and to carry in a full milk canister. She be a wee woman. The Moldens be good to me and others. No one around here would do this."

Cowan said, "We should have a look and perhaps ask the local sheriff or constable to send word to the Moldens."

Mr. Wells retrieved the key, which Cowan accepted. "Bow Street's investigations go beyond London," he explained, as a reminder of his authority. The locals did not have a need to know that Cowan was no longer a member of the force. Within less than a minute, they stood in a house strewn with broken pottery and furniture. Their only light was the lantern Mr. Farrin had fetched from the carriage box.

"What has occurred?" Darcy asked while standing awestruck by the scene's chaos.

"Someone has fought a fierce battle in this house," Cowan announced. "Mr. Wells, if you please, sir, fetch the local authorities in charge."

Disorder in the Crime

A soft snoring told George all he needed to know. He had lain awake to stare up at the shadows on the ceiling for more than an hour. What he was considering was not an action he could justify. It was one thing to cheat at cards or to woo a comely woman. It was another to commit a crime against another person. He knew what his father would think of this moment. "Always bowing and scraping for what old Mr. Darcy presented him," he murmured as he screwed his eyes shut to drive away the image of his father's constant disappointment. "A man has his scruples."

Yet, George knew if he was the type of person to lash out against another, this was the prime opportunity. A purse full of coins. An inebriated man. A house on the outskirts of town. No witnesses.

At length, he rose to stand looking down upon the waning fire. As if a puppet on a string, he slowly turned towards the dark sleeping quarters. His own fear was growing more and more ungovernable. "I could leave and no one would be the wiser. Schultz will wake in time for the ship or he will not. The man is not my responsibility. I should simply leave while I may," he told the room's silence. "Yet, I could escape England and start anew. Who says I cannot simply steal Schultz's purse and bag and be gone before he wakes? He never once asked my name, so he cannot connect me to the crime."

Turning slowly, he inched his way to the open bedchamber door. Step by step. Stealthily. He could hear the soft rasp of Schultz's inhale and exhale. George's future hung by a thread swinging in a light breeze. He glanced about the room to look for a weapon. "*Just in case*," he told himself. There was a broom. A wooden bucket. A variety of pots and pans. Then he noted a garden hoe in one corner, near the door.

George crossed softly to catch up the hoe in his hand. "*Knock him out with the handle.*" He balanced it in his hand. "*More sturdy than the broom handle.*" A silent weapon. "*Only use it if I cannot steal the items before he wakes.*" He looked over his shoulder to where nothing had changed in the room. A light snore said Schultz still slept. He crossed again to the room, though there appeared to be more loose floorboards this time than last, or perhaps he had not heard them previously.

He entered the bedchamber on silent feet. He did not know how long he stood there, still debating on whether to proceed or not. Just as he prepared to look around for the man's coat, where he suspected the purse was tucked away safely, Schultz shifted in the bed. George reacted by lifting the hoe to use as a weapon. For the briefest of seconds, he thought he might have awakened the man and wondered how he would explain his holding a handle above his head, but Schultz rolled over and tugged a small pillow to his chest before settling again. Meanwhile, George held on to the handle, counting the seconds in his head until he reached one thousand.

It was necessary for him to cross to the foot of the bed where the man's coat was folded and sat upon a chest. With the merest of movement, he edged ever so close to the coat. If he could reach it, he would simply steal the whole coat and not search for the purse. Men like Schultz always carried additional funds upon them, especially if they were traveling to a place where war surrounded, as it did in the Kingdom of Holland. He was ever so close to reaching out for the garment, when a floorboard snapped loudly from his weight. Schultz started up when he heard it, and George panicked. He swung the handle at Schultz's head, but the man's arm came up to catch part of the hoe with the intention of wrestling it from George's hand. Schultz used his weight and his position on the bed to push George backwards, and a mighty battle of wills began. George had expected the man to be still a bit inebriated, but not so. He stumbled backwards to slam hard against the wall, as Schultz rained down a string of curses, each echoing through the house, along with several punches to George's midsection.

A table overturned. The metal mug was knocked to the floor, its contents splattering across the floor and wall. Schultz had the handle of the hoe across George's neck, pressing against it, closing off George's ability to breathe. For a second, he thought it might be best if he surrendered to his fate, but then he thought of the pleasure Darcy would know with his passing. He had no idea why he considered Darcy at this moment, except he knew the man searched for him. Likely his old nemesis would testify that Schultz was justified in George's death.

Gathering his strength, George caught the handle a second before he raised his knee to strike Schultz in the man's privates. Effectively relieving the pressure on his throat, he ripped the hoe from Schultz's now loose hold and began to strike the man over and over and over. Even when Schultz was bent over and using his hands to protect his head, George's arms came down again and again in an indiscriminate manner. When the handle broke, he tossed the short end aside and struck Schultz repeatedly with both the broken handle and the hoe itself.

His chest heaving with a mix of exhaustion and the thrill of victory, at length, he stood over a bloody and broken figure. George threw the handle into a corner of the room, for Schultz no longer moved, and George assumed the man was either unconscious or dead. Truthfully, he preferred the former, but their encounter was over.

Realizing he must make haste, George turned his attention to Schultz's belongings. He grabbed the purse from inside the coat's pocket, for he knew it contained crowns, guineas, shillings, and even a roll of pound notes. Catching up the coat, he ran his hands along the lining. Two secret pockets were sewed into the material. He tossed it over his shoulder. There would be time to examine it carefully later.

Another glance to Schultz said the man had not moved. George, too, stood motionless as he looked upon the havoc he had wrought. Instinctively, he backed out of the room, leaving the scene behind. He should see to Schultz's body. Remove it from the house. But there was no ready means to do so, and George was not of the mind to drag it across the yard and down the small lane to the main road. He felt guilty for creating such havoc in an innocent couple's life, but not guilty enough to do anything to reimburse them or clean the house.

Instead, he sat in a nearby chair and tugged on his boots. As he began to gather his meager belongings, he caught up his own coat. He could not leave it in the cottage, for then the world would know it was him who killed Schultz. Instead, he fished out a pair of scissors from a drawer in a table and began to cut the coat into pieces so he might toss them into the fire. It was not easy to cut the heavy material, and he recited a string of curses as he pulled, tugged, and cut away the sleeves and collar and the lining. The wool in the coat had smoke seeping into the house itself, and he rushed to open a window on opposite sides of the room so the smoke could escape. He had thought to cut off the buttons to sell, but they were too hard to dislodge, and time was ticking away. In the end, he gathered up the coat and crammed it into the bag belonging to Schultz. George would be rid of it in an alley or toss it overboard once he was out to sea.

Afterwards, he entered the kitchen to claim a jug to fetch water to put out the fire once the coat was burned thoroughly. He had pumped the handle several times to prime it and began to fill the jug when, miraculously, Schultz stumbled out the door, pure rage on his countenance. Evidently, the battle was not yet won.

Realizing Schultz had to be weakened by their previous entanglement, George rushed the man. He caught the fellow by his shirt points and drove him backwards into the kitchen. They both landed hard on the floor. Arms and legs entangled, he half straddled the man and rained down a series of punches about Schultz's head. A cry of anguish filled the night, and, though George knew they were well removed from town, the shrieks of anger and pain brought him more fear than losing the fight to Schultz. He grabbed a cloth hanging from a drawer knob and jammed the end of it into Schultz's mouth. More and more. Handfuls of it. Until Schultz struck him hard on the point of George's temple and, for a few brief seconds, things went black.

Order in the Investigation

With Wells's speedy retreat, Cowan led the way. Though the residence was now lying in shambles, it was evident the Moldens held great pride in the house and the land around it. "Do not touch anything or move it, but have a look around to determine whether Wickham was actually here or whether someone else took advantage of the Moldens' absence."

Darcy and Mr. Farrin moved off in opposite directions, with Darcy easing towards the open door to the single bedchamber. He stood very still until his eyes adjusted to the muted moonlight streaming through the small window. "Appears to have been some sort of confrontation in here," he called. Immediately, Cowan was behind him and handing off a small candle he had lit from Mr. Farrin's coach lantern when they first entered the house.

His friend led the way into the room. "Be aware of where you step." While Darcy remained closer to the door, Cowan deftly stepped over and around the chaos within. "A small trunk," Cowan pointed to the other side of the bed. "Have a look inside, Darcy."

"What is that on the floor in the corner?" he asked as he moved to do as Cowan instructed.

Cowan stepped over the bedding and an overturned bowl and jug. "Some sort of broken handle." The man held his candle high and ran it down the length of the rounded wooden stick. "Broken. Hopefully, we will discover the other half in another room."

Darcy had worked the latch free on the trunk. "Men's clothing. A shaving brush. Extra blankets. And such."

"We will assume someone was in a confrontation in this room, and I want a closer look at the wood handle and the overturned mug after we have searched thoroughly. Whatever was in the pint pot does not smell of water or beer. Somewhere between spice and medicinal."

Darcy mused aloud, "As bad as is the air in London these days, I am surprised your senses can smell anything but filth."

"Mr. Darcy!" Farrin called.

Darcy followed Cowan out of the bedchamber and into the kitchen. "Dear God, what has occurred in this room?"

"Appears to be the end of what began in the sleeping quarters," Cowan murmured. "Watch your step. Blood can be slippery. Moreover, I want to preserve the footprints."

Darcy stretched out his stride to reach the other side of the freestanding cabinet. He expected to view a body upon the floor, but none existed. "I found the other end of the handle. Appears to be a garden hoe. Farrin, see if there is another lantern in the coach's box. We need more light."

"Aye, sir."

With the driver's exit, Cowan said, "Do me the courtesy of examining the barn. Lots of blood about. Whoever lost it did not go far." Darcy nodded his agreement. "Have your gun at the ready before you enter the barn. Take Mr. Farrin with you. I mean to have a look outside for tracks. I want to mark them as I did at that incident in London when the colonel was accused of murder. Whoever our victim is cannot be far from death or is already dead. As the ship sailed on Thursday morning, it has been at least two days since this confrontation."

Motioning Farrin to follow him, Darcy performed a search of the barn, even climbing the ladder to examine the loft. He admitted, though only to himself, he was not built for this type of drama. Before exiting the barn, he claimed another lantern, which was hanging on a nail, and found both a sulfur-tipped match and a tinderbox on the tack room's shelf to light it. Through a small window in the room, used to provide light, he spotted Cowan doing a search of the house's exterior. Returning to the main door, he called, "There is another lantern inside. Should I fetch it?"

"Nothing unusual outside the house. Not even footprints in the flower beds to indicate whoever created this scene had looked inside first. It is as if the person already knew something of the house, just as Mr. Wells told us. There is a blood trail across the kitchen threshold and possible drops on the stones."

"Take this lantern. I will claim the other one. It will not be light for another three hours or so." Darcy handed off the lantern and returned to the barn for the other. When he stepped out into the yard a second time, he heard someone calling for Cowan. Within seconds, Mr. Wells appeared, leading another man towards the house. Therefore, Darcy hustled across the yard to join Cowan, where his friend had paused.

"The constable, sir," Mr. Wells said on a rush. "Mr. Purdue."

Cowan extended his hand to the man who had been following closely on Mr. Wells's heels. "Thomas Cowan, sir. Bow Street." He handed the local law officer a card. Darcy assumed they were from the ones Cowan had used when he was still one of Henry and Sir John Fielding's men, offering more prestige than Cowan's own investigative office.

The constable studied the card, but Darcy was confident the man could not read Cowan's name in the dark. "Mr. Wells says you were looking for someone he previously saw entering the Moldens' house." The man presented Wells a disapproving look. "Now, I'm made to understand the Moldens' home has been turned on its head."

Cowan gestured to the still open door. "You are welcome to examine the house yourself. My associate and his driver," he gestured to Darcy and Farrin, in turn, "and I were searching for an army deserter, who also has accumulated a number of debts, causing more than a handful of complaints."

The constable appeared a bit suspicious, but he led the way into the house. The man remained silent as he moved cautiously from room to room, while Darcy, Cowan, Farrin and Wells waited by the open door. "I've never seen the like," Mr. Purdue admitted. "Naturally, I've seen my fair share of fights and about a half dozen murders."

"Would you permit my observations?" Cowan asked in humble tones.

"You personally know the man you suspect of this?" Purdue gestured to the scope of the room. "Is he capable of such a crime? Though, in truth, we do not know anything more than theft has been executed in this house."

Cowan nodded to Darcy. "Darcy here was raised alongside the man for whom we are searching. The fellow is married to Mrs. Darcy's youngest sister. We are very familiar with him. His commanding officer reported him missing from his duties. Word was sent to my friend, and, for the sake of his wife's family, we have been searching for the man."

"Does the 'fellow' have a name?" the constable asked.

"Wickham. George Wickham," Cowan replied. "We are aware of several hundred pounds owed in debt. Earlier, we learned Mr. Wickham shared drinks with a Mr. Jacob Schultz at an inn near the docks. Mr. Schultz is related to the Grose family, jewelers to King George himself. We also know Mr. Schultz departed on the *Le Lion du Nord* early yesterday morning. However, we do not know if the man on the *Lion* is the real Jacob Schultz or Mr. Wickham pretending to be Schultz. We will not know the truth with any certainty until we find both men. In my opinion, one of those two has committed murder, or, at a minimum, made a bloody attempt at it.

"With your permission, I would like to examine the scene while you and Mr. Darcy search for either the murderer or the victim. I likely have more experience in such matters. There is a trail of splattered blood leading across the kitchen floor and over the back door stoop. I was about to begin a search when you arrived. Follow the trail. With it being so dark, you'll require the lanterns. As you well know, sir, you must look for dark blood droplets."

From the look on Purdue's face, he had not considered following the blood droplets as part of the investigation, but the man wisely said, "Perhaps I should stay with you and Mr. Wells can assist your friend."

"As you wish," Cowan returned patiently, though Darcy knew his friend wished to be rid of the constable. Cowan was a very singular man when it came to a crime scene. "Would you be willing, Mr. Wells?"

"I've no gun, but I kin use a club if'n you have a true need of me."

"You'll likely not be required to search far, Darcy," Cowan warned. "Send Mr. Wells back if you find either Wickham or Schultz. Do not permit anyone else to touch the body until I examine it."

With a nod of understanding, Darcy departed out the front and circled the house. Wells and Farrin scrambled to catch up with him. "As Mr. Cowan said, we must look for drops of blood. The pavers are likely to show more than the dirt. Attempt to walk in the grass so as not to smear whatever we discover," Darcy instructed. "Mr. Cowan will want to know at which angle the blood spattered. He is the most knowledgeable man I know for this sort of business."

Wells and Farrin were both bent over at the waist and carrying the lantern close to the ground. "Your Mr. Cowan be a learnt man. You know each other long?"

"Not as long as I would like," Darcy admitted. "Cowan served with my cousin Fitzwilliam in the war."

"Does this look like blood to you, sir?" Farrin asked.

Darcy knelt beside his man and held his light so they might see better. "I think you may be correct, Farrin. We must assume if someone is injured, the blood would drop every three to five steps, do you not think?"

"I've no 'pinion, sir," Wells admitted. "Never much thought on it."

"That's the way with animals," Farrin agreed.

"Let us claim a few twigs and mark this one and then continue our search."

They worked well together, finding a line of droplets on the left-hand side of the path. However, when they reached the barn, Darcy sent Wells along the right-hand side of the structure, and Mr. Farrin out further so they could cover the entire area.

Darcy had chosen the path on the left, for when he climbed up in the loft earlier, he noted an open field and a tree line beyond. Whether it was Wickham or Schultz they followed, Darcy assumed the tree line had to be a closer route to the docks than the "twisty" way they had traveled through the town to reach the Moldens' house.

"Anything, sir?" Wells called.

"Let us cross the field," Darcy called back. "Keep each other in sight. Study the land. Look right and left. The field is still fallow, which will make it easier to spot a dragged foot or where someone stumbled."

They started forward together. Methodically stepping. Looking. Lifting lanterns to shed light on the process. Concentrating hard upon the task at hand. At length, Wells called, "There previously be no vines growing on the Moldens' stile!"

Darcy looked up to view something propped against the stile.

"Practice care in your approach," he instructed, yet, there was no need, for when Darcy reached the spot, his lantern proved the man's identity. "Fetch Mr. Cowan," he told Wells.

"Shudn't we lay him out first?" the man objected.

Darcy shook off the idea. "Not until Cowan views him. Cowan can tell how this ties into the scene in the house simply from viewing the body. The man is a genius in that regard."

"Yes, sir." Wells rushed off to do Darcy's bidding.

"Look around, Farrin. See if there is a weapon or some other tracks, but do not touch them."

"Aye, sir."

Meanwhile, Darcy knelt before the figure a second time to look upon a face he knew well. He had shared the breaking of bread with this man. Unfortunately, there was nothing he could do but offer a silent prayer for the man's soul. Within a minute, Cowan was running across the field. "Did any of you touch him?"

"No."

"Excellent. Hand me your lantern, Wells. Darcy, hold yours above the man's head."

"What do you hope to find?" Purdue asked as he stumbled to a halt to stand with the rest of them. The man was quite heavyset and not as agile as was Thomas Cowan.

"How many times he was struck. Angle of the blow. Was he bent over and attempting to protect himself with his hands." Cowan barely lifted the man's hand. It showed multiple cuts and lacerations. "See what I mean?" Purdue nodded his head in agreement. "Likely his back and sides are covered with what remains of bruises and other cuts." Cowan leaned over the body for a better look.

Meanwhile, Mr. Farrin returned. "No other footsteps in the ploughed field, Mr. Darcy. If anyone else be about, he left along the path leading to the main road, not through this stile."

"Thank you, Farrin. Add your light to assist Mr. Cowan," Darcy instructed.

"Look here, Purdue," Cowan said, very much appearing to ignore the news Mr. Farrin shared, but Darcy knew otherwise. Cowan possessed the type of mind to process it all. "The scalp is cut here and here and here." Darcy's friend used a pencil he had removed from his pocket and used it as a pointer. "Blood seeped out at one time, but now it is simply scabs. We will be able to tell more once we get him to the undertaker or surgeon—whoever handles these types of situations in Norfolk."

Again, he pointed to each example. The man was teaching Purdue to be a better observer in solving crimes he may face in the future. Ironically, the earlier brusque-mannered Purdue had disappeared. He was now an apt student. Just as was Darcy, Farrin, and Wells.

"That be what killed him?" Purdue asked.

"Injured definitely. Likely seriously, but, unless he was struck in a vital organ or bled inside, it was not enough to kill him. I am under the persuasion that this is a result of what occurred in the kitchen. The encounter began in the sleeping quarters and progressed to the kitchen. He was beaten repeatedly; yet, if I am correct, the beating did not kill him."

"How...?" Purdue began his question.

"Easy enough." Cowan stepped around the body to study the victim's countenance. "Shultz?" he asked Darcy.

"Been more than eight years since I encountered the man, but I believe it is Jacob Shultz. Most assuredly, this man is not George Wickham," Darcy confirmed.

Cowan stood to speak to Purdue. "The bedroom and the kitchen speak to us of a great struggle occurring within the house. It is my learned estimation Mr. Schultz was first attacked while he slept. The condition of the bed linens speak of an unexpected ruction, and the blood droplets say Schultz was struck at least twice while he was in the bed."

"I agree," Purdue said with self-importance.

Darcy knew Cowan fought the smile rushing to his lips: His friend had easily won the battle of who was in charge of the investigation. "And we agree Mr. Schultz managed to rise from the bed to continue the confrontation."

"Aye, sir."

"We also assume, the other man involved in this pother thought Mr. Schultz to be incapacitated, but, evidently, Schultz did not drink the beer prepared for him."

"The amount of beer on the floor and wall indicates as such," Purdue announced.

"And the smell Darcy and I encountered upon entering the room?" Cowan prompted.

Darcy looked to Purdue for the explanation. "We think it was laudanum. There be a bottle in the pantry and the cork be loose," the constable said.

"Parts of a military coat remain in the house, though someone appears to have cut it up and tossed the pieces in the fire to destroy it. Unfortunately, wool does not burn, but rather ignites briefly and then chars. It shrinks from the flame, curling slightly as if in an effort to escape the fire. Wool produces a strong odor, resembling the smell of burning hair, which is likely why we found the windows open on opposite sides of the sitting room to create a cross draft. The residue of what does burn completely turns into a black, hollow irregular-shaped bead that can be easily crushed between a person's fingers into a gritty black powder."

"We dug through the ashes and found a sleeve. An epaulette. Some buttons. It appears someone dragged several half-burned pieces out of the fire and across the hearth. Must have carried off the rest. Could not find them," Purdue explained.

"Obviously, Mr. Wickham must have attempted to burn the coat," Darcy surmised. "But would that not also mean Schultz was dead before Wickham escaped. How did his body end up slumped over this stile?"

"I will explain momentarily if you do not figure it out for yourself," Cowan assured. "But, first, assist me in placing Mr. Schultz on the ground, face up."

"What's ye hope to learn?" Wells asked.

"We must discover the murder weapon," Cowan said with a grunt as he lifted Schultz's upper body. "I will require the lanterns, and, Mr. Purdue, if you will assist me with Mr. Schultz's lips, it would be much appreciated. His body hardened almost immediately, but such usually only lasts for two days, which is how long Schultz has been hanging over the fencing."

"Can we not close his eyes?" Wells pleaded.

"In a few minutes," Cowan insisted in distraction. "I will require those tweezers I handed you earlier, Darcy. Have them at the ready."

They all looked on as Cowan wedged his fingers between Schultz's lips. "Assist me in opening the mouth, Purdue. Take the lower jaw."

The two men opened Schultz's mouth as if it were a trap set for a fox. In time, Cowan was satisfied. "We can have a better look when we move him into the house," Cowan instructed as he put his fingers in Schultz's mouth and searched it thoroughly. "Do you have a handkerchief, Darcy?"

"Aye."

"Open it and you and Farrin hold it taut."

Darcy set his lantern on the ground and did as he was instructed.

Within seconds, Cowan placed a wad of strings on the white cloth. "Likely more further down his throat. The tweezers?"

"In my breast pocket," Darcy directed.

Cowan fished the tool out of Darcy's jacket. "See. A few strings still remain between his teeth."

"I be damned," Purdue swore. "Would never have thought to look there. Could they match the cloth in the fire?"

"I hold no doubt," Cowan confirmed. "There are also a few in the blood smears on the kitchen floor. I believe Mr. Wickham thought, quite literally, to smother Mr. Schultz to death, though the dastard did not realize Schultz would pass out before he could actually die. If Wickham had left the towel in Schultz's mouth and then covered the man's nose with a pillow or something to prevent his taking a breath without swallowing part of the towel, Schultz would have been found on the kitchen floor.

"Instead, Mr. Wickham, for some unknown reason, pulled the cloth from Schultz's mouth and attempted to burn it, along with his coat. Part of each survived, connecting him to Schultz's death. If he'd thoroughly burned both and done away with the metal on the uniform and dumped the cloth overboard, no one could connect him to the crime. Naturally, we must confirm whether all these elements are accurately analyzed, but we can all assume Mr. Wickham is the man on the ship to Europe. With your permission, Darcy, I would give pursuit."

"I would travel with you," Purdue stated. "I shan't have anyone committing murder in Norfolk and not paying the price."

Though Darcy did not desire Wickham's return, for Elizabeth would worry for the future of her foolish youngest sister, he said, "Naturally. I will stand your expenses also, Purdue, and, once the investigation is complete, I would employ you to clean the Molden house properly and repair the broken furniture and the like, Wells. If you are willing, that is."

"Gladly done, sir. Thank you for the employment."

"Let us document the rest of what we discovered so Mr. Purdue has a solid case against Mr. Wickham and can move forward on his arrest."

Order All Around

Darcy noted the familiar handwriting on the letter on the salver Mr. Nathan set on the corner of the desk. Before he reached for the letter, he instructed, "Would you ask your mistress to join me, Mr. Nathan?"

"Yes, sir."

Darcy retrieved the letter. If the news was bad, he wished to be in a position to support Elizabeth. Breaking the wax seal, he unfolded it to read:

Darcy,

I know you have long been desiring this information, and there is much to explain, but know Purdue and I finally located Mr. Wickham. As you can well imagine, a confrontation ensued. The result was Mr. Purdue shot Mr. Wickham, killing him. The gun and the bullet were close to the man's head and blew away a part of Mr. Wickham's face, so the identification was more problematic than I had hoped; yet, I am confident the man was Mr. Wickham.

The former lieutenant was living in an area of Amsterdam only those of ill-repute would occupy. Whatever he stole from Schultz had been lost at the gaming tables abroad before we found him. Ironically, he still wore a coat of the nature the innkeeper and the man's patrons had described for us as belonging to Schultz. Because Purdue shot Wickham, we will be detained for another few weeks, perhaps a month before the local government will see fit to permit our passage to England. Yet, I knew you would wish to prepare Mrs. Darcy's sister for the official notice of her husband's death.

1. *Cowan*

"No problem regarding Mrs. Wickham," Darcy said to the empty room. "Elizabeth and I placed the woman on a ship to Canada last week. Hopefully, she and the child she carries will finally know peace. At least now, if Lydia 'Gardiner' wishes to marry again, she will be free to do so," he murmured. "By the time we learn where she has chosen to settle in the provinces and Mrs. Wickham is informed of George's passing, the child should be born. I pray it is a daughter so the girl does not remind Mrs. Wickham of her first husband for the remainder of her days. Elizabeth's sister has not the temperament to handle the news gracefully or discreetly. All we can do is to hope she has traveled to one of the provinces where the men outnumber the women a hundred to one. Lydia Wickham would thrive in those conditions."

Elizabeth appeared at the door. "Talking to yourself, Mr. Darcy?"

"In that manner, I win a few of the arguments," he said with a smile.

"You wished to speak to me, sir?" she asked with an arched brow.

He rose. "Yes, my dear. Come join me. I have heard from Cowan, at last."

~ Finis ~

Author Note: *If you enjoyed how astutely Mr. Thomas Cowan solved this crime, then you might also enjoy his role in a couple other of my award-*

Regina Jeffers writes books about corsets, rakes, daring heroines, dashing heroes and all aspects of the Georgian/Regency era. She is an award winning author of cozy mysteries, historical romantic suspense, and Austenesque vagaries. Jeffers has been a Smithsonian presenter and Martha Holden Jennings Scholar, as well as having her tales honored by, among others, the Daphne du Maurier Award for Excellence in Mystery/Suspense, the Frank Yerby Award for Fiction, the International Digital Awards, and the Chanticleer International Book Award.

Before writing romance, Jeffers wore many hats, including that of a tax preparer, journalist, choreographer, Broadway dancer, theatre director, history buff, teacher, grant writer, and media literacy consultant for school districts and public television. Now, "supposedly" retired, she writes full-time, skillfully enveloping her readers in the hearts and minds of her characters.

Readers May Find More from Regina on ...
Every Woman Dreams (Blog) https://reginajeffers.wordpress.com
Always Austen (Group Blog) https://alwaysausten.com/
Facebook https://www.facebook.com/Regina-Jeffers-Author-Page-141407102548455/?fref=ts
Twitter https://twitter.com/reginajeffers
Amazon Author Page https://www.amazon.com/Regina-Jeffers/e/B008GOUI0I/ref=sr_ntt_srch_lnk_1?qid=1479079637&sr=8-1
Pinterest https://www.pinterest.com/jeffers0306/
BookBub https://www.bookbub.com/profile/regina-jeffers
Instagram https://www.instagram.com/darcy4ever/
You Tube Interview https://www.youtube.com/watch?v=vzgjdUigkkU
Regina Jeffers Website https://rjefferscom.wordpress.com/

DEATH AT THE RACES

BY RIANA EVERLY

"My word, what a crowd this is!" Mary Bennet spun in a slow circle, taking in the carnival of sights and noises that surrounded her. "Not even in London on market day have I seen so many people in one place. And we are to stay here the entire day?"

Her brother-in-law, Fitzwilliam Darcy, nodded gravely. "The races are always popular, and here at Epsom Downs, more so than anywhere else in England. The purse is rich this season, and many come as much to see who wins or loses their fortune as to see which horse triumphs."

"It hardly seems like the sort of event you enjoy, Darcy." That came from the man to Darcy's opposite side, his broad Scots accent a contrast to almost every other voice Mary heard.

When first they had met, she had found his Glaswegian tones rough, almost incomprehensible, but of late, she had come to like them more than any others in the world. Likewise, the mop of copper-red hair that now shone about his head like a gaudy halo in the bright spring sun, Mary preferred to every other shade. Indeed, she had come to like Alexander Lyons far more than a lady of her sensibilities ought, and she did not mind it one bit.

They were here at Epsom Downs at the request of one of Darcy's oldest friends, Sir Edgar Moore, who owned one of the contending horses. Darcy had, at first, rejected the invitation, then glared at it on his desk for a week, and at last, at his wife's cajoling, agreed to take a small party with him as they cheered Whitehock on to victory.

And quite a party it had become! It began just with Darcy himself, his wife, Elizabeth, and his cousin Richard Fitzwilliam. Upon further consideration, he had invited his friend Alexander, his cousin Anne de Bourgh (along with her companion, Mrs. Jenkinson), and, of course, Mary, who was staying with the Darcys in London. Then, at Epsom, they had come across more of Darcy and Sir Edgar's circle, and their families and entourages, and before Mary could spell her name, there were more than twenty people all gathered about the area close to the track that Sir Edgar had reserved for their carriages.

"Care for a walk, Mary?" Elizabeth asked some minutes later, coming up from where she had been talking to new acquaintances. "We are not so far from the grandstand, and see there, by the clearing? Mrs. Farringdale says there are stalls where one can buy hot Chelsea buns and every other manner of food and drink. We can watch acrobats and visit fortune tellers, as well. Do come. Perhaps we might find presents for Mama, Kitty and Lydia."

"Fortune tellers, acrobats, and thieves, my dear," Mr. Darcy added. "Take only what you must and stay vigilant."

"Will you join us, Anne?" Elizabeth asked. But the lady was sickly and preferred to remain behind.

"You should go, Mrs. Jenkinson," Anne urged her companion. "Sitting here with me cannot always be amusing, and my cousins will be fine enough company. Mrs. Alcott seems a pleasant sort as well, and she might wish to remain here."

The ladies were about to head off when a sudden roar interrupted the pleasant hum of their gathering, and a wild-looking man crashed through the wall of carriages. His face was obscured by a large hat that shadowed his features, but his voice boomed loud.

"Moore!" the man thundered. "Where are you, you rat? They said you were here. Come out and face me!"

The murmur of conversation ceased at once, to be replaced by a series of stifled cries and gasps at this most unwelcome interruption. Near Mary, Mrs. Alcott sucked in her breath and muttered something, while across the circle by his carriage, Mr. Darcy called out, "What is this? Explain yourself!"

"Moore knows who I am," the belligerent interloper shouted. "I see you there, cowering like the scared rodent you are. Stand tall and face me like a man!"

Sir Edgar bowed politely to the woman he had been conversing with and stepped forward, shoulders back. "I am facing you. Who are you, and what do you want?"

"You know exactly who I am, you rat! And what I want is my money. You owe me plenty of it, and not a penny have I seen. I demand payment, and I demand it now. If you have enough blunt for your pony, there's plenty then to give me my due. Or else!"

"Or else what?" Sir Edgar asked, inclining his head.

"I'll tell them all! I'll tell them all about the games you've played to get your winnings. They'll like that, they will. This crowd won't take well to cheaters. You pay me, or you will regret it!"

Mary held her breath as Sir Edgar levelled a cool gaze at the wild man. He clearly knew now who this person was.

"I owe you nothing, and your stories are just lies. Get yourself away and bother somebody else."

"I'll have you, Moore... I'll be at the shed by the stables at three. You're there with the money, or I'll tell the world how you've cheated."

With that, he ripped off his hat, flung it to the ground and spat on it. Then, as if only at this moment realising he had an audience, he turned slowly about, staring at everyone in turn. When, at last, he faced Mary, he froze, his eyes growing wide. And then, with no warning, he let out a strangled cry and stormed off as quickly as he had arrived.

The stunned silence lasted just a moment before every voices erupted in gasps and exclamations of shock and amazement. The men let out oaths, and Colonel Fitzwilliam looked ready to run after the man, until Darcy stayed him with a hand on his shoulder.

Mary took in the scene as a tableau, committing it to memory: Elizabeth's hand covered her mouth; Anne de Bourgh was as pale as snow; Darcy clenched his jaw; Mrs. Farringdale seemed about to laugh; Sir Edgar, now that his foe had run off, looked quite shocked; at Mary's side, Mrs. Jenkinson swayed on her feet. And Alexander stood perfectly still, watching the proceedings with wide, interested eyes.

"Who is he?"

At Alexander's question, Sir Edgar swivelled around, his face drained of blood. The baronet had retained all the poise and command of his station while the madman was raving, but now he appeared as shaken as the rest of their group.

"He seems a difficult fellow. I have some experience in these matters, if you will talk to me," Alexander added.

Darcy nodded. "I introduced Lyons to you as my friend, and that he is, but he is also an investigator, and an excellent one at that. I trust him with my life."

The young baronet cast his gaze from Alexander to Darcy, then back again, before taking a breath.

"Yes. Very well. It cannot hurt to tell you, although I hardly recognized him at first. He has gone quite mad." He glanced about at the others and then indicated with his head. "Walk with me while I look in on Whitehock. He is in good hands, I know, but I would see him." He began walking in the direction of the stables, and Alexander and Darcy followed.

"You would hardly know it from his appearance now, but he is a gentleman by birth. Lucas Pritchard, the judge's son, if you have heard of him. I cannot say exactly what happened, but one moment he was the darling of the ton, and the next he vanished in a dark cloud of mystery. There were rumours of a scandalous attachment, of family heirlooms going missing, of witchcraft and even devilry, but I cannot put any credence to that nonsense. What I do know, because I had the man investigated when he came to me about two years ago, begging for employment, is that he disappeared many years ago with no word of his whereabouts, not even to his intended bride, for they were engaged to be married shortly thereafter. I suspect he fell in with a bad crowd and owed far too much money to the wrong people."

Alexander looked up in surprise.

"A strange story indeed, is it not?" Sir Edgar tutted. By now they had reached the stable near the shed that Pritchard had mentioned. They entered and spent a few minutes marvelling over the magnificent racing horse that occupied most of his stall. Alexander knew little more about horses than the average man, but even he could see that Whitehock was exceptional.

At last, satisfied with the beast's wellbeing and the comfort of his trainer and jockey, Sir Edgar continued. "Whatever had happened, Pritchard knew racing. He knew all the trainers and breeders, and he knew which horses were strong in which areas, and which were weak. He knew who was running where, who the jockeys were, and how to fit into the network to the best advantage. With his knowledge, I was able to get Whitehock into the winner's circle more than once. We made a penny, we did, and I paid Pritchard well.

"Then he changed. Perhaps he began wagering again. I do not know. But his information became less accurate and after a time I had to bid him farewell. The last I heard, he had wagered on another horse and blamed me when Whitehock won. Said I had cheated, and that I owed him his winnings. I did nothing but engage an excellent man to train a fast horse to the best of his ability, and carefully select the field."

"What of his intended bride? Could she tell you nothing?" Alexander asked.

Sir Edgar shook his head. "Miss Matthews, she was. No joy there. She was nowhere to be found. Rumours, again..." He sighed before speaking on. "You know what rumours are, most of it nonsense. But she, too, disappeared from London soon thereafter, and has not been heard of since. From the lack of hue and cry, I believe her disappearance was contrived by her family and is not alarming. Still, we have no answers from that quarter."

Alexander nodded. "Why come to you now, and in such a bother?"

Sir Edgar merely shrugged. "Perhaps he owes more money to the wrong sort. The sort that might make an example of someone who cannot pay."

Darcy, who had been silent until now, spoke at last. "What will you do about him?"

"I shall meet him at three, as he requested," the baronet asserted, "but he shall have no joy from me. He can rant and rave all he wants. I owe him nothing and will not succumb to extortion."

With that, he strode ahead of the others, back to the circle of carriages where their party were preparing to watch the next race.

The others had not been idle, and the space they had been allotted, so close to the fence demarking the racing oval, was busy still with all manner of activity. Chairs had been arranged for the ladies who wished to watch the race, some with convenient parasols propped nearby, and food and drink were being set out on small tables. This all must have come on the carts that had accompanied the carriages, with the small army of footmen and endless baskets of food. Had Alexander been alone, he would have been happy sitting on the muddy ground with a piece of cheese and a tankard of ale.

The carriages were now arranged so the men could climb to the roofs, there to enjoy the spectacle, while the servants scurried around in response to this request and that command. It was a beehive of activity, and if not for the shadow that Lucas Pritchard had cast, it would have been a merry gathering indeed.

But the time for musing was over, for the race was about to begin. Darcy and Elizabeth sat together inside one carriage with the door open so they could watch. Colonel Fitzwilliam and Mr. Farringdale perched atop Darcy's carriage, and Anne de Bourgh with her companion took two of the shaded chairs near the side. Mrs. Alcott and another woman whom Alexander had not met were in two of the other chairs, and a group of men sat on the roof of Sir Edgar's carriage. That man himself stood by the fence, waiting. His horse was not in this race, but he was deeply interested in it, nonetheless.

And then there was Mary, standing alone in the shadow of Darcy's conveyance. Alexander grabbed a blanket from a pile and spread it out on the ground in invitation. She answered with a beautiful smile, and they both sat down together, a moment to themselves in the midst of this whirlwind of activity.

Then, at last, the race began.

A moment of silence, followed by a roar, and the horses were off!

After the bated breath and the blur of racing equines, there was time to converse. Mary told Alexander of her morning, of trying to talk to Anne de Bourgh, of Elizabeth's new friendship with Mrs. Farringdale, and of the strange stare the wild man had given her.

For his part, Alexander informed her of the man's name and history, as much of it as he knew, and of his thoughts about Pritchard's threats.

"He might have no substance at all to his claims," Alexander explained, "but if there is even a whisper of Sir Edgar being dishonest, his reputation will be in tatters, as will his fortune, for everything he has relies on his horses."

"Then one must hope," Mary replied, "that he is able to satisfy his foe and not allow the accusations to be voiced too loudly."

All too soon, the race was over, and the members of their little party began to move around once more. As some of the ladies gathered to discuss a stroll to the booths, the colonel leapt from the roof of the carriage, landing in a patch of mud and splattering several skirts. Mary looked down in distress at her frock and groaned, while Elizabeth chastised her cousin-by-marriage and Darcy looked on with a wry grin. It was good to see Darcy happy in his choice of bride. The man was too serious at times, and Elizabeth's cheerful teasing had brought a lightness to him that suited him well.

"It will dry, dearest," Darcy soothed her. "It is only mud, and we are certainly not the only souls so afflicted. We are at the races, after all, and I recall a time when six inches of mud on your petticoats caused you no bother at all! My cousin is suitably chastised, and no doubt will attempt to make amends with treats for all the ladies." With smiles and laughter, the group separated for the time being, with expectations of gathering again before the final race, when Sir Edgar's horse would strive for the lead.

Alexander spent a few minutes talking to Mr. Farringdale and the colonel before glancing at his pocket watch. Nearly three o'clock. Sir Edgar had not asked for his presence, but he would go to the shed regardless, in case of trouble. At the gesture, Colonel Fitzwilliam raised an eyebrow, a sign that he would come as well. Alexander knew the colonel and respected the man, even if he was a bit afraid of him.

They reached the shed shortly before the hour. Alexander had not seen Sir Edgar before them, but he was surely nearby. Perhaps he had been here earlier, still. The door was open, and Alexander strode forward. Only silence greeted him. Good. Perhaps neither adversary had yet arrived. But wait—

"Hush!" The colonel shoved Alexander aside and flung himself to the side of the door. He dropped down to a crouch and shifted so he could see inside.

"Bloody hell!" he exclaimed, leaping to his feet and barging inside, Alexander on his heels.

On the floor, with a massive slice removed from his head, lay the body of Lucas Pritchard. And standing over him, looking quite green, was Sir Edgar, a bloody shovel at his feet.

"I swear, on everything I hold dear, he was dead when I walked in," Sir Edgar all but sobbed. He was still shaking, even half an hour later when Alexander at last had a minute to talk to him.

Colonel Fitzwilliam had taken charge at once, yelling for help, securing the room, and finding someone to sit with the dazed baronet. At his request, Alexander had examined the body as best he could without touching it, with the understanding that a coroner and the local magistrate must be found as quickly as possible. Even without his smattering of medical knowledge, it would have been easy to discern that the instrument of death was the shovel lying by the body, its blood-stained blade exactly matching the deep wound on the dead man's head.

Who had wielded it was a different question, and the one Alexander was now posing to the man found with the victim. "I was angry, I admit, but I never... I could never... I did not kill him!" Sir Edgar declared and clamped his jaw shut.

At first glance, it appeared he was telling the truth. His clothing was pristine, his cravat blindingly white and perfectly tied, his light summer coat uncreased and lying smoothly on his shoulders. The effort taken to swing a spade hard enough to kill a man would surely disarrange his clothing, and there was no sign of blood—or anything else—on his crisp cuffs. Still, he was known to have had a disagreement with the dead man and was found with the body. Questions must be asked, and by those with more authority than an officer on leave or a private investigator.

Horrified and sick at heart over the senseless slaughter, Alexander dragged himself back to the gathering of carriages. Mary saw him from a distance and hurried to meet him partway.

"What happened?" she asked. "It must be bad. I know you too well to think otherwise."

"Murder," was all that he was able to say at first. Then, as Mary stifled a gasp, he found the rest of the words. "Lucas Pritchard is dead. Killed. They have kept Sir Edgar aside. He was found with the body."

An ordinary young woman might swoon at such rough words, but Mary was no ordinary lady. Meek and insignificant-looking at first glance, her face held a quiet beauty that had quite spoiled him for anything else, and her mind was as sharp as many a brilliant man's. If she had been granted a proper education, she could have eclipsed them all. Moreover, she was observant. And right now, what she saw was the pain in his heart.

Nor was she a stranger to such violence, having helped him solve more than one such crime in the past. She was, as the cant went, made of tough stuff. He could talk to her. In as few words as possible, Alexander recounted everything he knew and had seen, pausing only when Mary asked one of her astute questions. By the time they staggered back to the carriages, she knew as much as he about what had transpired.

"If it were not Sir Edgar, then who?" She wrinkled her nose in befuddlement. "I suppose that is for us to discover."

"Now, Mary, it might have been any one of the tens of thousands of people here today. Epsom is not known for its calm atmosphere and the sophistication of its spectators. The very person Pritchard was afraid of might have been the one to swing the shovel. Or some drunkard, hoping for coin and disappointed."

Her raised eyebrow asked if he truly believed his words. Once more, she was correct. "But yes, I feel it is someone closer to home. And not Sir Edgar."

Retrieving the rest of the party from their peregrinations was hopeless, and they must wait for their companions to return of their own accord. With the final race coming soon, they did not have too long to wait before, one at a time or in small groups, their circle wandered back.

There, past the circle of carriages, Darcy and Elizabeth walked together, gazing at each other with eyes that should not be permitted in public places. Mrs. Alcott and Mrs. Farringdale returned a moment afterwards, each with a large bag of treats procured from the stalls. The men strode back laughing, with Mr. Farringdale trailing the others by a minute or two, and then, at last, came Anne de Bough and Mrs. Jenkinson, the older woman dabbing at her sleeves and Anne's shawl with what looked like an old cloth.

"Oh, that mud!" the companion declared when they arrived at last. "I shall never get Miss de Bourgh's petticoats clean, and Lady Catherine will be most displeased. One must be careful not to displease Lady Catherine."

"No, indeed." This was almost the first time Alexander had heard Anne speak. "Mother is quite firm in her opinions and expectations."

Alexander approached Anne first. "I am afraid I must bother you for a moment," he said, damping his Scottish accent as best he could. "Where have you been this last while? There are no wrong answers, but I must know for... something I am looking into."

"Oh!" Anne placed a thin and pale hand on her collarbone. "Whatever has happened? Mrs. Jenkinson helped me walk to the stalls to find some honey lozenges I had heard somebody mention. Mrs. Alcott, perhaps, when we were sitting together earlier."

"Anything more?"

"No, indeed. I sat for a while to gather my strength, and then we returned. Would you like a lozenge? I hear they are good for the throat."

Mary's eyebrow twitched.

"Thank you, but no. Your frock?" Alexander gestured to the mud-spattered hem, the stains thicker at the bottom and lightening until they disappeared around her knees. Not that a man ought to contemplate a lady's knees, even in the course of an investigation.

"I do not think it so badly ruined, but we have attempted to clean the worst of it. Mrs. Jenkinson is more concerned than am I." She held out the cloth Mrs Jenkinson had been using, and he took it. It was old and well used, with the vestiges of some embroidery at the edge, now damp and dirty with smudges and the grey mud that they had wiped on it. Alexander took it without a word.

"Thank you. Please do not leave this area for a while. I may need to ask you more."

"Oh, indeed not! I am quite done in."

Alexander handed the cloth to Mary, who peered at it and then placed it on the floor of the Darcys' carriage.

Next, they spoke to the Darcys, who had been walking together, but never out of sight of the footman who was watching the carriages. They had nothing of import to relate and could not have been involved.

Mrs. Farringdale grinned as they approached. She seemed to be enjoying the play, even if she did not yet know what had happened backstage. She was not the sort to be easily shocked, and Alexander began with his strongest statement.

"Pritchard has been killed."

Instead of crying out or collapsing and calling for her salts, the lady sat forward, eyes alert and interested. "He has! What an interesting outcome. Shocking, rather, but— Oh, do tell. What happened? I must know."

Mary cleared her voice and responded. "He was found in the shed where he was to meet Sir Edgar." She omitted the details of weapon, injury, and main suspect. Alexander could always trust her.

"How thrilling. Am I to be questioned? I would rather like that. It will be something to tell the ladies at tea. Pray, Mr. Lyons, what are your questions? I shall answer them all honestly and thoroughly."

And she did. She and Mrs. Alcott had also gone to the crowded grounds with the stalls and tents. Mrs. Alcott wished to have her fortune read, and there were many people there plying that trade.

"Did you go in with her?" Mary asked.

Mrs. Farringdale gave a moue. "Alas, Madame Gipiti did not permit it. I had to stand outside the tent while she did, well... whatever it was she did. Come, let us ask Eleanor now."

"And did you go anywhere while you were waiting?"

"No, and more is the pity. I was the next in line, but before I could take my turn, my husband and Mr. Alcott chanced upon us, and we all went in search of lemonade. It is warm today."

Mrs. Alcott's account matched her friend's precisely, with the addition of reporting that the fortune-teller was a charlatan. Their husbands, too, had been together the entire time, looking at the horses, until they encountered their wives and went to find something to drink.

At last, having questioned every member of their party, Alexander led Mary to some chairs near the edge of their area and threw himself onto one. Mary followed suit, although more gracefully.

"We have spoken to each person, and not one had anything to tell us." He sighed. "Unless..." He turned his head to find someone in the group, and Mary followed his gaze.

"Yes. I think I know who it was," Mary whispered. "And I might know why."

"Miss de Bourgh," Mary ventured, "may I ask one further question?"

"Please." Anne was no conversationalist, but she was nothing like the domineering presence that was her mother.

"When you rested, after buying your lozenges, how long did you sit?"

The frail woman thought for a moment. "It was not a very long while, but more than a moment. I was entertained watching the acrobats and did not think to measure the time. It was perhaps twenty minutes, certainly not more than half an hour."

"Thank you. Ah, your handkerchief. I retrieved it from the carriage where I left it. It looks well loved." Mary held out the old cloth.

"Oh, no, that is not mine. It belongs to Mrs. Jenkinson, who uses it when she would rather not soil something new."

Mary nodded. "Very well. I shall return it to her myself. Thank you."

She returned to Alexander with a sad smile. "I believe we are correct, although I take no pleasure in it."

Alexander bowed his head. "I concur. Shall we, then? Let us round up our prey."

In short order, a much smaller group were gathered behind the carriages, where they were somewhat hidden from curious eyes.

There were chairs for Mr. Darcy, the colonel, Elizabeth (for she would not be denied), Alexander, and Mary. And, of course, for their suspect.

"We know it was you," Alexander began. "If you confess, we will do everything in our power to ease matters for you. Perhaps a time in an institution for the mad, or transportation. I know some excellent barristers who will work hard to keep you from the gallows."

"The evidence is compelling," Mary added. "If we were able to learn this in just an hour, a judge will have no difficulty in discovering the truth. Please, admit your actions."

"An innocent man is now being questioned for a crime he did not commit. If some pig-headed magistrate takes it into his head that Sir Edgar is guilty, you will have killed two men. Have a conscience and confess." That was Mr. Darcy, in his sternest manner.

At last, Mrs. Jenkinson lowered her head and let out a shuddering breath. "Yes. Yes, already. I killed him. But he deserved it, for what he did!"

Mr. Darcy's shoulders relaxed, and the colonel's face twisted into a grim smile.

"Now, Miss Mary," the colonel asked, "will you explain to the rest of us how you knew?"

"There were several small details that together painted a picture. The first thing, although I did not understand it at the time, was the reaction the deceased had to Mrs. Jenkinson. When he looked at us all in turn after making his strange speech, I thought it was me he was staring at. But no, it was Mrs. Jenkinson, who stood right beside me. He knew her, and by her response—for she nearly swooned— she knew him as well. I suspect it was not a pleasant reunion.

"The next piece was Anne de Bourgh's statement. She told us that she and Mrs. Jenkinson had gone to seek the lozenges together, but said, '*I* sat for a while,' and then '*we* returned.' That suggested she had been sitting alone. On further questioning, we found that Mrs. Jenkinson had been gone for nearly half an hour, ample time to slip into the shed and confront Mr. Pritchard.

"Then there were the stains on Mrs. Jenkinson's clothing. When you leapt from the carriage and splattered us with mud, Colonel, the dirt was found on the bottoms of our skirts, near the hems, and certainly no further than our knees. But Mrs. Jenkinson was dabbing at stains on her sleeves. Stains that might have come from swinging a heavy shovel at a man's head."

That lady let out a sob, but Mary continued.

"As Miss de Bourgh's companion, she must be strong, for Lady Catherine surely has her carrying and fetching all day, little motions that build great strength. But her biggest weapon was her anger. You see, Mrs. Jenkinson was the woman Pritchard abandoned all those years ago, effectively ruining her life."

"Indeed!" The colonel was most interested now. "How did you determine this?"

"That they knew each other, and were not pleased to see one another, was the first clue. But I also have this." Mary drew the old handkerchief from her reticule. "This is yours, is it not, Ma'am?"

Mrs. Jenkinson nodded but said nothing.

Mary held up the corner, bringing attention to faded embroidery. "HM. It is embroidered with the initials HM. These are not your initials. Or, rather, not your present initials. I cannot say what the H is for, but the M, I surmise, is Matthews. You were Mr. Pritchard's betrothed."

At last, Mrs. Jenkinson opened her mouth to speak.

"He said he loved me. We were to be married, and I... I allowed him liberties. When I discovered I was with child, he had disappeared without a word. I was sent to the country, where I took on the persona I now use. I claimed I was the widow of an officer lost in battle, with no family and no hopes. I could not afford to keep my baby, and he was adopted by the local parson and his wife, who had no children. I begged for a chance to teach at a small village school, and then found a position as a governess. No one knew the truth, and for so long, that has been who I am. I have my present position with Miss de Bourgh on the strength of previous recommendations. If Lady Catherine learns the truth, she will send me off without a penny. Lucas... Lucas knew who I was. I could not risk having him speak my name, or worse, threaten me with exposure if I did not fill his purse. I had to do it. He destroyed me once. I could not stand to have him destroy me again."

The colonel extended an arm to the weeping woman. "Come, madam. Let me escort you to the magistrate, who I believe is talking to Sir Edgar even now. And then, with luck, Sir Edgar can return to us in time to watch his horse run to victory."

The two walked off, one leaning heavily on the other's arm, and Mary stepped closer to Alexander. Here, shielded by the large carriage, no one would see her press softly against his side, or notice his arm snake around her waist to pull her close. The truth had been found, but there was little joy in it. Murder was always a sad business.

The End

If you enjoyed this story, be sure to read **The Mystery of the Missing Heiress**. *This free novella introduces Alexander Lyons in his first adventure with Fitzwilliam Darcy.*

Riana Everly is an award-winning Canadian author of Austenesque fiction, both Regency and contemporary. Her historical mystery series, **Miss Mary Investigates**, has quickly become a favourite of Jane Austen fans and cosy mystery fans alike. Trained as a classical musician, she also has advanced degrees in Medieval Studies, and pretended to be an academic before discovering that fiction doesn't need footnotes. She loves travelling, cooking her way around the world, playing with photography, and discussing obscure details with her husband and children. Possibly in Latin.

She can be found in the usual places and loves connecting with readers, so please give her a shout!

Newsletter: https://form.jotform.com/80367829232259
Website: rianaeverly.com
Email: riana.everly@gmail.com
Facebook: facebook.com/RianaEverly
Instagram: instagram.com/RianaEverly
Amazon: amazon.com/Riana-Everly/e/B076C6HY27

SHADOWS AT NORTHANGER

BY JEANETTE WATTS

"Well, I do not think it is right, I do not. Kicking those monks out. They were not doing nobody no harm."

"The king thinks otherwise, so you had best keep your mouth shut."

"The king is not the one moving here."

"The new family is friends of the king. Probably GOOD friends, or they would not be getting one of the biggest abbeys in Gloucestershire."

"This is the only abbey in Gloucestershire, you lout."

Margery could hear the workmen grumbling as they hauled in the family's effects. The crates of clothing and other personal effects took up several wagons, and should have arrived well before the family; but the rain which had made travel difficult for the family carriage had made it impossible for the heavier wagons.

It was not the most auspicious arrival at a new home for the

Daubeny family. The journey had been long, and cold, and wet, and they had only the clothes they were traveling in. On the other hand, the caretakers knew of their arrival, and had prepared fires in the fireplaces, hot food, and proper beds for all of them that night.

In the morning, the weather had cleared and Margery and her sisters were able to explore their new home before breakfast.

There were still construction projects everywhere. The room where they slept had been altered from the monks' small sleeping quarters into modern roomy chambers, but there were several other bedrooms still to be completed. There was no need to make any changes to the grand wooden staircase they had sleepily climbed the night before, and of course there was no need to update the kitchens. Monks ate well.

When they entered the great hall, very hungry from their morning's explorations, they found another hall with little need for alteration, although their father immediately took issue with the tapestries.

"I think your first order of business is to send for something suitable from Brussels, Margaret," he commented as they ate. Both parents, the three sisters, and their younger brother all spent the meal unable to sit still, there was so much to see.

"Of course, Edward," their mother had answered. "I will send for them immediately."

There were large changes needed, like the tapestries, and small ones, like the crucifixes found in a cabinet. There were indoor changes, like the bedrooms, and outdoor changes, like the gardening. The spring weather was the perfect time to plant the beds in the quadrangle with roses and lavender, and replace the statue of the Virgin Mary in the center with a fashionable knot garden.

The gardens elicited more grumbles from the workmen. "No. No, no. I'm not touching it. What kind of curse is going to fall on a man for removing a statue of the Blessed Virgin? No good is going to come of it…"

Margery was enjoying a walk around the grounds on a dry day a couple of days later, glad to finally be reunited with *all* her clothes. Of course the gardeners wanted to take advantage of the same fair weather. After wandering farther afield, she was reluctant to go inside, and she went into the quadrangle to admire the new beds and the work in progress. This put her in a position to overhear snippets of the arguments in the garden, although they were quickly stifled as soon as the men realized she was there.

They forgot all about her a couple moments later, however, when one of the men pulled his spade out of a section of newly turned dirt and a naked arm came out of the ground with it.

A lot of yelling, and movement followed, and no one noticed Margery when she crept closer to get a better look. It was a man's arm, hairy, with a large hand at the end of it.

One of the workmen approached with another shovel, only to be pushed aside by his mates. "Are you daft? Do you really want to dig it up in pieces?"

"We're going to dig it up? Shouldn't we be burying it?"

"Well, we need to find out who it is first."

The men were on their hands and knees, using their hands to scoop away the dirt. The arm was attached to a shoulder, which was attached to a torso, and a neck, and a head. The entire body quickly emerged.

They stood in a circle around the body. No one even commented as Margery stepped boldly up to stare with them.

The body was entirely naked, slightly rounded, not terribly tall. The face was also round, and the head was bald.

"One of the brothers here!" someone gasped.

"Do you recognize him?"

"Well, no, but look at that head."

"Me grandfather's bald like that, but he never been a monk," another workman snorted.

"Well, you explain who he is."

"How does one contact a monastery that has been disbanded?"

Margery asked pragmatically. "Surely one of the brothers will recognize their fellow brother."

All the workmen now turned to stare at her, seeing her for the first time.

"Coo, milady, you should not be here." One of them reached out to take her arm, then looked down at his grubby hand and thought the better of it. Margery was glad of that; she loved her new gold brocade dress. The dark brown fur trim might not have shown the dirt as much, but she really did not want to find out.

"Well, I am here, and I can tell my father you've found something in the garden, and we need to contact one of the monks," she offered.

They looked at her a trifle uncomfortably.

"I won't tell them you allowed me to gaze upon a naked man, if that is what you are worrying about," she promised. "I have seen parts before. I have been to London. I have seen men relieve themselves."

"Well, I suppose we ought to tell the master that we found a dead body in his garden," the one who had found the body in the first place answered.

Margery decided, as the daughter of the lord and lady of the estate, it was time for her to take command. "You gentlemen stay right here, I will fetch him." After all, she knew her father was looking at marriage projects on her behalf. She would be the lady of her own estate sometime soon. She needed the practice.

As she turned and lifted her skirts to run up to the main hall, she heard the workman who had found the body exclaim in an awed voice, "Coo! Did you hear that? She called us gentlemen!"

She nearly fell over from laughing and stepping on her own skirts. She lifted them a little higher. It might be undignified, but it would be more undignified to be sprawling on her face in the dirt.

After running through the large peaked entrance, she stopped and assumed a gliding walk. She liked to amuse herself by walking on her toes, so that it looked like she was floating over the floor. Her mother did not care for it, and thought she looked bewitched. Her father liked it immensely and claimed it made her look more graceful than any other lady in the room. Margery calculated it was better for her to impress her father than her mother. And her mother would not scold her for running if she was gliding smoothly over the stone floors.

Four rooms of fruitless searching later, she gave up and found one of the servants. They always knew everything. One was not supposed to ask the servants anything directly, but Margery was past caring about the niceties. "Sarah, I don't suppose you could give me a suggestion where my father might be?"

Sarah looked up from her broom and dustpan. Margery forced herself not to giggle at the alarm on the maid's face as she dropped everything and dropped in a courtesy. "Have you tried the stables, Lady Margery?"

"I have not. Thank you, Sarah."

Not caring anymore about looking graceful, Margery resumed her run. Down the wide staircase, back out the grand entrance, take a right, down the path, around the hedges, she was out of breath when she reached the stables. And there stood her father, inspecting horses she did not recognize with the head groomsman.

"Father," she blurted out, knowing she would get a lecture on manners, but not caring, "There's a commotion going on in the quadrangle you need to investigate. There's a dead body!"

He took off running. Margery's father was a spry man. He had to be, to maintain his position as one of the king's favorite jousting companions. It took a lot of athleticism to lose at jousting, be thrown from your horse in a full suit of armor, and not get injured. It was the reason the king elevated the family, and why they were now enjoying this beautiful new home – that had a corpse in the middle of the garden.

She ran after him, not trying to keep up. Her legs were so much shorter than his; and if she were not running with him, he was less likely to tell her to go away and not follow.

The workmen and the body were still there, mostly as she'd left them. Someone had thought to clean the mud off the dead man's face, and they were standing around staring at him, puzzling over his identity.

Margery was close enough behind her father to hear him as he approached the group. "What have we here?"

The workmen all bowed. Her father gestured with his hand for them to recover, then they all began speaking at once.

"The tree came in for the knot garden."

"We was moving Mary, here, and the dirt was already kind of soft by her feet."

"I put the shovel in, but he still has all his parts. Even his arm is still whole. I found his arm first."

"He must be one of the brothers. But I been here at the monastery for a long time and his face is not one I know."

"How can he be a brother if you don't know his face?"

Her father held up a hand, and they all stopped. Margery hoped she could do that someday. Not with her husband, of course. But when she became the lady of the manor, she wanted to be able to command others with a gesture, the same way her father did.

In the quiet, he knelt down and touched the body. "He has not begun to decompose yet. He has not been dead long. The dirt here was already soft? When did you begin working on this part of the quadrangle?"

"We started the roses a week ago, maybe."

"We started the lavender first, but no one was near Our Lady Mary."

"It was two Sundays ago since we started digging the flower beds."

Her father stopped them all again. "Never mind. More importantly, we need to find out who he is. None of you can identify him?"

They all shook their heads.

"Hopefully one of our neighbors can be of assistance. You lot carry him to the infirmary and get him cleaned off, while I send out to some of the neighbors. All of them have been here for quite some time, I believe." He turned and looked directly at Margery. "Go collect Agnes and Catherine. If the three of you ride to our northern neighbors, the groomsman and I can ride south to our two southern neighbors."

Everyone in the courtyard scattered to their assignments.

Margery wrote out notes for her two sisters, who were less excited than she was about the errand.

"What if we get murdered while going to deliver the message?" Agnes asked.

"If you think you need the protection, take two grooms with you, instead of one," Margery shrugged. "Who is going to kill a harmless girl while she is out for a ride on a beautiful day?"

Catherine shivered. "The same person who murdered a harmless monk and buried him in our garden."

"Monks can't be that harmless," Margery reasoned with them. "If they were so harmless, why did the king take away their monastery? They must have done something wicked."

"Now I definitely want two grooms," Agnes answered. But she mounted her horse and went.

It was an exhilarating ride. For all her brave words to her sisters to bolster their courage, their fears transmitted to Margery. What if they were right? There was a murderer somewhere nearby. There was a murdered body right there in the quadrangle! That was very close. There could not possibly be any danger to her; her father would not have sent them out on this errand if there was any danger. Or perhaps he simply did not think things through, in his eagerness to get an answer. She was glad she had followed her sister's caution, and taken two grooms with her for protection.

Being the eldest and the best rider, she had elected to take the longest ride upon herself, all the way out to Sudeley Castle.

She had been so focused on the dead body, writing the notes, getting her sisters underway, and staying close to her grooms while watching for murderers on the winding roads through the Cotswold

Hills, she had not thought much about what she was going to say when she reached her destination. As they trotted up to the intimidatingly sprawling walls of the castle, she remembered only now that King Henry and Queen Anne had been here only recently. What was she going to do if they were still there? The thought thrilled her – and terrified her. It was one thing to see the king from across a jousting field while her father was present. Quite another to enter his home uninvited.

Fortunately there were no royal standards flying above the castle, which meant she only needed to apply to the housekeeper or groundskeeper.

The groomsmen dismounted, and by the time they helped her from her horse, three people had emerged from the house to stare at her.

In her haste, she had not changed into her riding habit, and was still in her gold gown with the brown fur sleeves. No doubt she made a very strange sight to the servants of a royal household. She dropped her shoulders and lifted her chin. Well, she wasn't riding all the way back home to change her clothes right now.

"Are you lost miss, or have you run away from home?" the elderly woman in the center of the welcoming group asked. Surprised, Margery looked into her face more carefully, and was relieved to see a smile lurking about the corners of the woman's mouth.

"Neither, madame. I am Lady Margery Daubeny. My family has recently taken possession of Northanger Abbey."

The hint of a smile faded from the woman's face. "I see."

"There's been a murder at the abbey. The workmen found the body of a man buried in the garden. They think he might be one of the monks, but they don't recognize him. My father sent me to ask if someone from the castle here might be willing to come tell us if they can identify him. We don't even know how to find the monks who used to live here. My father is hoping one of our neighbors might know. If the man is one of them, they ought to know."

The woman looked her over appraisingly. "The king might not approve of your family talking to the monks from your abbey."

Margery stared back at the woman. The thought had not occurred to her, and she didn't think it had occurred to her father, either. "If this man is indeed a monk, and the king wanted him dead, my father will do with the body whatever the king tells him to do," she answered uncertainly. "We just need to know who he is, so we know what the appropriate course of action is."

The woman's face softened a little again. "Go home, girl," she answered. "I will... send someone from the staff here who might be able to put a name to your mystery corpse. What does he look like?"

Margery described him as best she could. The woman nodded. "You've delivered your message, you have just enough time to get home before dark."

"Thank you, madame." Margery wasn't sure where she stood in relative rank to the woman, but she dropped into a courtesy anyway.

The ride home seemed to take half as long as the ride to the castle. The woman's stern demeanor puzzled Margery a little. Her father was on good terms with the king. Excellent terms. Such excellent terms that the king gave her father Northanger Abbey. But the woman's unfriendliness was not what Margery would call neighborly.

All thoughts of the neighbors, royal or otherwise, fled her mind when they reached the stables. Her father, and mother this time, and the groomsmen were all standing just inside the stable doors, all staring at the ground.

Margery felt a chill spread through her arms and legs when she realized they were all staring at another body.

She was out of her saddle and on the ground before her grooms could dismount and come to her aid. "What did I miss?"

Her mother turned around at the sound of her voice, and Margery found herself wrapped in a smothering embrace. "My darling child!" She felt a kiss planted firmly on her forehead. "I can finally take a breath again. I cannot believe your father sent all three of his daughters riding out all over Gloucestershire when there are dead bodies about."

Speaking of dead bodies! Margery wriggled out of her mother's grasp so she could see the new one. "We all took two grooms along for safety, Mother." She looked over the new arrival. "At least this time we know he's a monk." He was lying face down, and he was covered in mud and manure, but there was no mistaking the ring of hair with the bald pate, and the coarse cloth of a monk's robe.

Two of the grooms turned him over, then took a rag to wipe off the face. She gasped. "That's not a monk. That's one of the workmen from this morning!"

"None of the workmen shave their head like a monk," one of the grooms disagreed.

"None of the workmen were wearing monk's robes, either, but there he is," Margery answered.

He father stared at the face a long moment, then into Margery's eyes. "Are you sure?"

Margery looked at the dead body again, took a breath, and confessed, "I might have come and talked to them for a bit before I left to come find you. He has blue eyes and his hair used to be a bit longer. And – he had hair on top of his head, this morning."

The dead man's eyes were closed. Her father gestured to the skeptical groom, who knelt down to lift an eyelid. The eyes were blue.

Her mother shivered and turned away. "Come, dear, you had a long ride. The grooms are taking care of your horse; I should take care of you. You need some fresh clothes, and I can see on your face this adventure has not spoiled your appetite. Your sisters have already returned, and should be sitting at the supper table by now." She gently took Margery by the shoulders and guided her away from the scene. "Edward, shall I make up a plate for you?"

"I won't be much longer. And yes, like Margery, I am still hungry."

Margery felt her mother's shudder through the hands on her

shoulders, and twisted to wrap her arms around her mother's waist. "It's going to be all right, mother."

"I hope so," she sighed. "I knew coming out here would be uncivilized. We are almost in *Wales*, after all."

Of course there was little else anyone wanted to talk about as they ate. Agnes and Catherine told their stories of their rides to neighboring estates, Margery told of Sudeley Castle and its unfriendly housekeeper. Their mother rolled her eyes repeatedly at the horrors of the three of them riding around the countryside when there was a murderer about. Their brother was disgruntled that he did not get his share of the fun.

"Sorry, you are still a bit too young to be sent out on errands alone." Agnes was only a couple of years older, but loved to lord it over him.

Before a squabble could get underway between the youngest two Daubenys, their father spoke up. "In all the excitement of the day, I have not had the time to confer with you, Margery. I had an answer to my correspondence, on your marriage project. Are you still certain you like the looks of the Earl of Kent?

Margery looked up in surprise. "Is *that* why you were asking me with whom I best liked dancing?"

She loved her father's smile. "Well, I can't have my daughter unhappy with my choice of husband for her. If you say you approve, my girl, the Earl has confessed he likes your looks, as well. I will settle the matter. I will write my letters tonight. It will take my mind off today's events."

The happy butterflies in Margery's stomach took away her appetite in a way that *two* dead bodies could not.

The morning brought no new answers. The workmen did not claim the second dead man as one of their own.

"No, never seen him before."

"His hands are too soft to be working in the garden."

"Monks also work in the garden," Edward Daubeny pointed out, giving them all a stern look. The lot of them shuffled their feet nervously, but none of them changed their story.

"Weren't there five of you yesterday? Where's the one who wielded the shovel?"

"That were me," one of them answered.

"Weren't you taller yesterday? I could have sworn the one who found the arm with his shovel came up to my nose." Her father looked him over with a critical eye.

"I had so much dirt on my shoes, I *was* taller," the man answered.

"That's a lot of dirt," her father commented dryly.

The men all shrugged. "We move a lot of dirt some days."

"The second dead man is one of them. I swear he is. The men must simply be afraid," Margery whispered to her mother.

"As you pointed out, there are two dead men. That strikes me as a good reason for staying quiet. Mind your tongue and follow their example," her mother whispered back.

When one of their messages to the neighboring estates succeeded in flushing out one of the previous inhabitants of the abbey, they were still none the wiser.

The former monk looked carefully at the first body, then made the sign of the cross.

"So, he's one of your brothers then?" her mother asked hopefully.

"No, my lady. But he has such a kind face, he is clearly a child of God, and I will pray for his soul," the monk answered.

"And this one? Is he not wearing the robes of your order?" her father pointed out.

The monk looked into the second face and made another sign of the cross. "No, I do not know this man, either. The robes are very much like the ones we used to wear. Perhaps this man is a beggar who was happy for some simple but warm clothing, and someone who is embracing the king's edict with too much zeal decided to impress the king by killing a man of God."

They all stared at each other for a moment.

"Do you know how the king wants to handle burials, now that he has dissolved the monasteries and is the head of the church?" the monk asked. "These men are still dead, and their souls still need tending to."

Her father shook his head, a puzzled frown on his face. "I don't know. I don't know what the rules are."

"Their bodies are starting to smell. We can't wait much longer to bury them," Catherine announced artlessly.

"Also an important consideration," the monk answered with only the smallest twitch to his mouth.

Their father sighed. "Well, something has to be done, and now. Would you please render last rites to these poor souls, whoever they are? And I will ask the workmen to handle their burials."

The entire Daubeny family attended the funerals of the two mystery men. They did not dare say a word in support of the monk's Catholic mass, but at least they were there to be mourners for the dead. No one should die without anyone to mourn them.

"These men might have families somewhere. I wish I knew whom to tell that they have lost a brother. Or a husband, or a father. Or a son," their mother murmured to Margery, as the youngest two Daubeny children put bouquets of wildflowers on both graves.

They were somber as they walked back to the abbey from the little graveyard. "I'm going to send some letters," her father told her mother when they were back inside. She merely nodded in response.

The mood lasted most of the day, but by supper, Margery and her siblings had regained some of their equilibrium. More of the servants and workmen had arrived, and the abbey seemed to be buzzing with activity as the great hall was measured for new tapestries, carpenters began working on more of the rooms, and more plants arrived for the gardens – along with more gardeners.

As everyone assembled for supper, their father did not appear.

"Margery, dear, would you go fetch your father?" her mother asked her. "He has a lot of correspondence, but he can resume after he gets a little something to eat."

"Of course." Margery was glad to get to run to the study. It was another one of the few rooms that was finished before they arrived, and the warm wooden panels still smelled a little of stain and varnish. She liked the smells; they were a promise to turn a cut tree into a different kind of beauty.

"Father? Mother sent me to fetch you for supper." Margery paused when she saw her father, asleep at his desk. She felt sorry for him; the ordeals of the past couple of days had taken a toll on him. She could see it was hard to be the head of the family.

She turned to tiptoe back out, using her hands to muffle the sound of her skirts. Then she stopped and turned back. Tired as he might be, he would still want some supper.

"Father?" As she walked beside his desk, she noticed the wine glass tipped over sideways, and that the papers under his hand were soaking wet. He was so tired, he had knocked over his wine and hadn't even noticed. Maybe she should let him sleep. No, she would encourage him to continue slumbering in his bed, instead of here at the desk. "Father?"

He didn't stir. A cold feeling started somewhere in the middle of Margery's stomach. "Father?" She put her hand on his shoulder, pushing him ungently. "Father?"

Still no response from him. She could hear her own voice rising in pitch with each iteration of the one word. "Father?"

Margery backed away, the cold feeling spreading. She needed to find someone before the cold reached her arms and legs, and she couldn't run for help.

There was no one in the hall, since everyone was assembling for supper. Supper! Hardly able to see, she ran the length of the corridor, and stumbled into the great hall. "Someone needs to go help Father," she blurted out stupidly.

There was a moment of panic when she thought no one could hear her over the collected voices of the household. But then there were footsteps, and a hand on her shoulder, and then more footsteps, and more hands. And then her mother was holding her, and weeping.

There was a lot of weeping.

Her father was buried in the same graveyard as the other two bodies; except there was a proper burial marker placed above him, so everyone knew that he was a father, and a husband, and a brother, and a son.

Since the family was no longer headed by the king's favorite jouster, they were soon asked to leave the abbey. No one voiced the least objection to leaving. The workmen continued their projects, but the family packed with great haste, relieved to be going.

"It looks peaceful from far enough away," their mother said as their carriage rolled away. "But no home ripped from men of the church will ever be a happy home. Northanger Abbey is going to be filled with wretched people for a long, long time."

The End

Jeanette Watts is a dance instructor, writer, seamstress, actress, and very, very poor housekeeper. With books on historical fiction, modern romantic comedy, LGBTQ romance, Jane Austen-inspired stories, and she is contemplating writing steamier works, what do all these genres have in common?

Jeanette writes about people with a secret. Secrets are fun.

Keep up with the various parts of Jeanette's brain at her YouTube Channel, "History is My Playground," and her webpages, Jeanette-Watts.squarespace.com and DancingThruHistory.com.

Instagram: https://www.instagram.com/jeanettewattsauthor/

Facebook: https://www.facebook.com/JeanetteWattsAuthor/

Twitter: https://twitter.com/JeanetteAWatts

Linked In: https://www.linkedin.com/in/jeanette-watts-3b212228/

YouTube: https://www.youtube.com/channel/UClz5LwyUEhPYhBS6piNpBqQ

Website 1: https://jeanettewatts.squarespace.com/

Website 2: https://www.dancingthruhistory.com/

Goodreads: https://www.goodreads.com/author/show/6967936.Jeanette_Watts

Amazon Author Page: https://www.amazon.com/stores/Jeanette-A-Watts/author/B00ICRA7JC?ref=ap_rdr&isDramIntegrated=true&shoppingPortalEnabled=true

DARCY'S REVENGE

BY MICHAEL RANDS

There are certain unexpected benefits to sleeping in your car. The morning light comes in through the windscreen and wakes you slowly from restless dreams. So, you don't need an alarm, that's one thing. Provided you sleep with the engine running, and the heater on, cars are toasty warm, so you don't need a blanket either. If you have a decent canister, and prep your drink the night before, you can take a sip of lukewarm coffee without having to get out of bed. And the view, well, that can be just about anything you want it to be.

In happier times his sister-in-law told him that if you count your blessings each morning, you'll realize how much you have. Like much of what she said, this had sounded like, if not quite drivel, then an unnecessarily sentimental take on life. But perhaps Jane had been onto something after all.

He took a sip of his—to be honest, cool, not lukewarm—coffee, and looked at himself in the rearview mirror. He resented himself for turning this phrase over in his mind, but he could not deny the essential truth of it: Life was not meant to have turned out this way. Not his life. What if one of his old acquaintances or friends were to walk past and see him, Fitzwilliam Darcy, living in his car, just another failed dreamer in the broken city of dreams, Los Angeles. Or, what if *she* was to see him?

"Elizabeth," he said her name, and then dared to imagine that at this very moment she was thinking of him, too, and thinking of him fondly. Remembering how things had been. Remembering him for who he really was.

Elizabeth hadn't wanted to leave the East Coast.

"I'm a Boston girl," she'd said to him.

He could not argue with that. She had only the slightest hint of an accent, but once you'd heard it you couldn't unhear it. Darcy, who spoke in a neutral Connecticut accent, loved to make fun of her when they first started dating. The first morning they woke up together he jokingly said to her, "So, we're going to get Dunkin Donuts now?"

"Yes," she said. "I'd assumed we would."

"Oh," he said, taken aback. "So, Bostonians, really eat Dunkin Donuts every day?"

"Not every day," she said, getting out of bed, and pulling on a pair of sweatpants. "That wouldn't be healthy. But going a whole week without eating there wouldn't be healthy either."

He'd been delighted to learn that she checked the full spreadsheet of Boston stereotypes. She came from a family that Darcy had imagined only existed in novels from the Kennedy era. Five sisters, two blondes (the elder pair), and a trio of entertaining, if slightly deranged, redheads. Irish Catholics, they still went to mass on Sundays, ate fish on Fridays, felt guilt over all manner of sins and lacked all intention of ever changing their behavior. In fact, the lack of desire for "self-improvement" which he perceived in Elizabeth's father was both horrifying and, somehow charming. Having grown up under the guidance of an intimidatingly accomplished father, he found Mr. Bennett's total satisfaction with his mediocre life, somewhat soothing. Her mother was neurotic, and gossiped all day, talking about her husband in front of him as if he weren't there. This too, didn't seem to bother Mr. Bennett. Her younger sisters traipsed in and out of the house at all hours, with friends and boyfriends, and occasionally rescued animals. The house was in a constant state of chaos, and although Elizabeth apologized frequently to him about her family, he knew that she did really love them all. Her mother she found difficult, and Darcy had not liked his would-be mother-in-law for quite some time, but as he got to know Elizabeth better, he came to understand that her mother had probably once been a highly ambitious woman, but unable to find a productive outlet for her energies had poured them all into the tragically futile pursuit of getting a man who had less ambition than the couch he spent most of his day on, to do something with his life.

As Darcy's own father had always reminded him, much of personality is genetic, and Elizabeth must have gotten her ambition from somewhere. For ambition she had. No, she hadn't attended Harvard. This was, naturally, the first question his prying aunt Catherine had asked him, when he told her about Elizabeth. They both knew that Darcy had gotten into the school, at least in part, because his family had helped fund the quantum trading department back in the early 90s, and the school knew they could "hit them up" as his aunt said, whenever they needed a new building or endowed chair. Yes, he'd had a perfect ACT score when applying, but so had half the applicants. Everyone knew you needed a little something extra to push you over the finish line.

Elizabeth had been at Boston University when they started dating and then she got accepted into Columbia Law School right at the time Darcy had taken his first job at his late father's hedge fund, Pemberley Capital. His father's will had stated that he must be given a job at the fund if and only if he graduated from Harvard and had not, "done grievous harm to the family name."

In Pemberley, Darcy was viewed with a combination of resentment, awe, suspicion, and at times, he suspected, fear. Here was the son of the founder of one of Wall Street's most legendary—and infamous—hedge funds. Darcy Senior had started the fund in his mid-twenties, and by the time he turned forty was a billionaire several times over. Bull or bear markets, it mattered not to Darcy Senior, Pemberley Capital *always* made money. When many of his peers were sticking guns in their mouths during the financial collapse of 2008, Darcy Senior was doubling his already astounding fortune. By the time the 2010s rolled in, Darcy was one of the wealthiest men in America. All the money in the world however did not save him when a group of Somali Pirates attacked his catamaran during one of his increasingly risky adventures.

In their two years in the New York apartment Darcy and Elizabeth went days, and once or twice, a full week, without seeing one another. She would stay at the library working till midnight, and he was sometimes required to sleep at the office. But when they did get to spend time together it was like floating in heaven. Sometimes they'd spend the whole day in bed, wrapped in sheets, making love. Other times they sat on their balcony drinking wine, reading to one another from whatever book or article they thought might take the other's fancy, or sharing opinions or beliefs they held which they would never share with their peers.

It was a difficult time in many ways, a time where a hundred-hour work week was considered a slow one, but they both felt alive, infused with purpose. The future seemed so present, so bright, and so certain.

Darcy was no simple man, and he knew that life was too complicated to ever find a single moment to point at, and say: this is where it all began to go wrong. But if he was forced to identify one such moment, it would be a Friday afternoon, in mid-summer. A beautiful day in New York City. He was planning to get off work in time to meet Elizabeth for dinner at some Thai restaurant she'd recently read about, when Thomas Bertram, the head of the firm, the man who'd taken over from his father, called him up to his office.

Bertram was an MIT graduate which, in his mind, made him far superior to Ivy Leaguers. "We do difficult stuff there," he'd say. "We don't sit around and talk." He had a PhD in applied mathematics, and was very deep into the whole "optimization" movement. While his birth certificate identified him as a 55-year-old, his "biological age" he claimed was 38 or—if you asked one member of his medical team—more like 36. Fasting, ice baths, supplements—the man did it all.

"Darcy," he said, getting up from his desk which stood in front of a glass wall overlooking Central Park. "I'm going to make this quick and easy. Take a seat."

Darcy did as he was asked.

"You and I both know you got this job because your father founded this place."

"I did have to meet certain other requirements, as, I assume you know, sir."

"Sir? What is this? Listen to me Darcy, I'm not here to give you a hard time. The fact is, you're good at your job. Damn good. You're easily the best in your cohort, and one of the best hires we've made in years."

"Thank you," Darcy said, trying his best not to fall for the flattery. Of the many lessons, his father had taught him, he remembered this one well: When a man blows smoke up your ass, fart it back out.

"It's a great relief to me, to tell you the truth. I didn't know how you'd be. It would have been a great disappointment if you hadn't had your father's tiger blood. But evidently, you do have it."

"I'm glad I didn't let you down." He tried to retain his composure, but the truth is, these words were like balm to a wound. He hadn't realized how badly he'd needed this kind of assurance. Elizabeth always told him he was doing great, and he did believe her, but the truth is, she didn't really know. Only this man here, really knew.

"You think you have tiger's blood?"

"My father used that phrase, too. He used it as if it were something absolute and objective. Some had it, he said, but very few."

"You're not answering my question."

"I believe I have it, yes."

"Good. Then I have another question for you. Have you heard of Bitcoin? Cryptocurrency?"

"I've heard of these, but I don't know much about them."

"To my mind it sounds like a load of horseshit, but my *opinion* is irrelevant. This firm has one job: to make money. And from what I can tell, there is money to be made in cryptocurrency. A whole shit-load of it. I'm hearing whispers that one day the industry could be worth trillions of dollars. If that's true, we cannot be on the sidelines."

"I agree."

"You're going to head up the crypto division of our fund."

"I..."

"Listen. I need you to move out of New York City."

"Why?"

"We claim to be contrarians in this firm, and yes we are, but the truth is, everyone in the industry claims to be a contrarian. And that, as you know doubt know, is an impossibility. Something your father knew well: if you want to think differently, you have to *live* differently. You can't be surrounded by people who all went to the same schools, and live in the same neighborhoods. I need you out of here."

"I have a girlfriend. We live together. I can't leave her."

"Make her your wife and head out west. Let me know Monday morning."

He showed up for dinner twenty minutes late—to make matters worse, his phone hadn't been working in the subway—and Elizabeth sat with her arms folded across her chest for the entire conversation.

"California, Fitz? Really?" she said. "I don't want to live out there. I don't like it there."

"Why?"

"The people are weird. My family is here!"

But that was the only time they ever argued about it. After that, they spoke, they discussed, they reasoned through, but they never argued.

Two weeks after that initial conversation he asked her to marry him, and the day after she graduated summa cum laude they got married on his family estate in Connecticut. A few weeks later she found a job at an environmental law firm, and a month after that they were living in L.A.

As fortune would have it, Elizabeth took to their new lives with greater ease than Darcy. She loved her job, and found that far from feeling out of place, she fitted right in. The culture was a perfect match.

"These people care so much about what they do. They understand there are higher values in the world than money."

"Good," he said. "I'm so glad you're happy here."

He knew that she didn't mean comments like that as a dig at him; she gave him endless encouragement and validation. But still, it would burn, just a little. It was then he'd hear his father's words: Money is the blood of civilization. Don't trust those who say they're in it for some other reason. They just haven't learned to be honest with themselves yet. Learn to be honest, brutally honest, and you can have anything in this world.

But he didn't dwell on these moments long.

This time, he now recognized, had been the happiest of their lives. They both wanted to wait to have kids, and so they could—for now, they always said—just enjoy one another's company. Elizabeth continued to thrive at her work, and Darcy found the world of cryptocurrency fascinating, if somewhat terrifying. It was, he came to believe, the wild west of finance. And it was in the frontier lands that men made their fortunes.

Being his own boss meant he could set his own times, and Elizabeth's work believed in the whole "work-life-balance" thing. They had money, they had time, they were young, and they lived by the sea, in a town of dreamers.

He returned early from work one afternoon, and turned on the television in their open plan kitchen, just to have something on while he made himself a smoothie. Flipping through the channels, he came across programming he would usually have flipped straight past: a man in a suit testifying before congress. Yes, he knew that tech leaders got dragged in front of congress once in a while to testify about this or that, but everyone in the industry knew that these old men were a joke. They didn't know the difference between a social network and a block-chain. But then he saw the tag on the screen: *George Wickham testifies before senate during Crypto hearings.* A barrage of thoughts entered his mind at the same moment: *oh yes, I heard about these hearings; oh yes, I'd heard there was a Wickham making waves in the crypto world…* And most loudly: *But I didn't realize—somehow, how?—that it was* This *Wickham.*

Not a minute later Elizabeth came home, her face bright.

"I saw your car in the drive, and I was so excited…" But then her countenance changed. Her face reddened, and she dropped her phone to the floor. "Why is that man on my television screen?"

"That man?" he said, pointing at the screen. "You know that man?"

"Turn that off right now," she said, marching across the room, and pulling the television unplugged from the wall.

Darcy knew his wife to be a woman of strong opinions, and fierce will, but he'd never seen her react like this.

"That's George Wickham," she said. "That man should be in jail not testifying in front of congress. In a suit. Like some kind of hero."

"How do you know this man?"

"I didn't tell you about this, because I… I don't know why. I didn't want to drag you into our family's *real* drama. But when my youngest sister, Lydia, was sixteen years old, that very man, took her off on some trip. They left the country together, and stayed in the same hotel room. She said, she swore, that nothing… intimate occurred between them, but I think she was just defending him. Why? I don't know. I tried to press charges against him, but it was futile. *Hasn't broken any laws. No evidence. No witnesses.* But I didn't have to dig too deep to learn that Lydia was not his only... dalliance. Let's just say Mr. Wickham prefers his women to be girls. He's into all kinds of disturbing stuff. Drug fueled much of the time. I don't want to talk about him anymore. If I never see or hear his name again, it'll be too soon."

"Shocking," was all he said. But he remembered the way Wickham had looked at Georgianna, his little sister, as she climbed out of the swimming pool that one summer day. He realized then that although he hadn't made this choice consciously, he'd gone to great lengths after that to keep the two of them apart.

No way anything ever happened there, right? He would have known.

But why, he wondered now, had he not told Elizabeth right then everything he too knew about Wickham? Was it just because she'd said she didn't want to talk about him anymore? That would certainly be the explanation that framed him in the best light, but was it true? He doubted it.

Although they had long since lost touch, Wickham and Darcy had been childhood friends. His father, Wickham senior was the foreman in the first building Pemberley Capital had been headquartered in, and Darcy's father had taken a real liking to the man. He said he was loyal and hardworking. His son—the man who now testified before congress—had also grown up in Connecticut, but not amongst the ultra-wealthy. Darcy was unique amongst his wealthy peers in attending the local public school. His father was certain it would breed a better character than some "private school bubble world." Wickham had been his classmate, and the two had spent countless hours exploring the impressive Darcy estate, and when old enough, sailing around the lakes. Mr. Darcy had left a provision in his will that granted Wickham the very same rights he'd granted his own son: he was to get a job at Pemberley Capital if and only if he graduated from Harvard and had not "done grievous harm to the family name." Wickham, needless to say, had not been offered a role at Pemberley.

It was not two months later that Darcy was up in the Bay Area for one of his frequent financing meetings. The rest of the crowd had left, and he planned to spend a few hours working alone in a coffee shop. That's when he heard a voice that immediately turned his blood to frost.

"Fitz? Is that you?"

He looked up from his work. "George?"

"It's me," he said, taking a seat opposite his boyhood friend. "I'd say we haven't seen each other in years, but I assume you've seen me quite recently, haven't you?"

"Where would I have seen you?"

"Still the naïve joker, huh, Fitz?"

"You mean that whole congressional thing. Yes, I saw it."

"I heard via the grapevine you were in crypto, too. You never reached out why?"

"I think you and I have different approaches."

"You've probably heard some things about me." He gave that famous, heartwarming grin of his. "Half of it's likely true, Fitz, I won't lie." He winked. "The other half? Well, a gentleman never tells. The point is, I'm not a saint, but I do know how to make money."

"OK," Darcy said. He desperately wanted the conversation to end.

"Crypto doesn't work like other assets. Your Ivy League education counts for nothing. You need information..." He looked over his shoulder. "Privileged information."

"You're just in front of congress the other day telling them you want to regulate the industry."

"Oh, and I do. Come on, Fitz. Remember what your father always told us. Be honest with yourself, even if you lie to everyone else."

"Those weren't his words."

"Close enough. This is America, Fitz. Surely you aren't so naïve.

The poor and stupid go to jail for breaking the rules. The rich and smart, we write the rules, so we don't need to break them."

"It's been good catching up with you, George. I hope everything goes well for you."

"Here's my card," Wickham said, as he stood up.

That evening Elizabeth could tell something was off with her husband.

"You're gazing into the distance, Fitz. Like you're not even here. What's up?"

"Nothing much. I just had a weird meeting this afternoon."

"Weird, how?"

"I sometimes wonder about this industry. There are some who say, oh, we're going to bank the unbanked, and save the poor, but do they believe it? Isn't it really just about making money?"

"There's nothing wrong with making money."

"No, of course not. I just, I don't want that to be the *only* focus of my life."

"It isn't the only focus of your life. I'm here, aren't I?"

"Of course. I was daydreaming about making enough money in this industry, that I could get out—with my own money, not inherited—and then do something really meaningful. Imagine if we could start our own NGO, or a fund of some kind. Make a real difference in the world."

"I love that idea," she said, taking his hand. "And if that happens, I'll be very happy. But I'm happy now, and I love our life. And if you're not enjoying crypto, you don't have to stay in it."

"I know I don't have to... technically."

She squeezed his hand, and he knew she understood what he meant.

The next few months were both turbulent and ultimately uneventful. Darcy and Elizabeth enjoyed married life, but he was not satisfied with his work. Increasingly, he came to feel like a man who'd arrived late at night at a casino, forced to play games he understood, at best, partially. One coin went up as another went down. The catalyst might be a tweet, or a new meme. And yet, every day, someone made out like a bandit.

Wickham appeared in front of congress again, proclaiming the new era of prosperity crypto would usher in, insisting on the importance of regulation, and reaffirming that he had to be the man to spearhead it.

Then came his second meeting with Wickham. It was at a conference hosted in the Bahamas. Lizzy had not been thrilled about him going, but she understood its importance. Wickham was the main attraction. He headlined several talks on the main stage and hosted the afterparty every wanted to get in to. Never having been one for wild parties, Darcy had planned to head back to his hotel right after the last session of the day. But while fixing his hair in the bathroom mirror, he heard the unmistakable voice of his old friend, and a moment later saw him standing there.

"Of course you're coming to my place, Fitz. You'll die when you see the view."

Was it curiosity that drove him there? Jealousy? Could he really be jealous of Wickham? The thought disturbed him. Whatever the case, he did attend the party. The apartment was quite unbelievable: the size of a hotel with twenty-foot-high windows that looked out over the ocean. There were drugs, and hookups, and girls who looked like they should have been at home studying for their ACTs.

Near midnight, Wickham put his hand on Darcy's shoulder, and led him to a private alcove that looked onto a patch of moonlit rocks.

"I'm going to give you this one for free, because you're my oldest friend," he said, writing down the name of a coin on the back of his business card. "Don't be an idiot, Fitz. Don't waste your life."

When he got back home two days later, he said nothing to Elizabeth about meeting Wickham. He mentioned the party and said it wasn't to his taste. She nodded, raised her eyebrows, as if she knew something.

A small portion of his funds he stored a folder named "batshit crazy." He'd yet to actually invest any of this money, but one Wednesday evening a week after his conversation with Wickham, he decided to place all of it—a hundred thousand dollars—on Wickycoin, the crypto his childhood friend had informed him of. Three months later he sold out, having made a thousand percent profit.

Elizabeth noticed a change in her husband during these months. He'd been buoyant and carefree one moment, as if life had written him a blank check, then anxious and avoidant the next. He checked his phone frequently. She woke at 2am one night to find him on the couch staring into his laptop, his face contorted as if he were having teeth extracted. But when he finally cashed out, a calm settled over him that lasted weeks. He slept through the night, made jokes at the breakfast table, took her out for surprise dinners, and doted on her like he had in their earliest days together.

With a single trade Darcy had met all his targets for the year, and in the weeks of his blissful repose—during which he devoted himself to his wife's happiness—he saw two clear pathways before him. In the one world he walked away now, content with what he had; in the other—oh, if he'd not met Wickham again so soon, this dark path could have been avoided—he kept going, returned to the table, unsatisfied with his status as a self-made millionaire.

"Billionaire," Wickham said, as he grinned at him across the table, his pearly teeth blood red in the moody light of Stan's Bar. "With a B. Anything less than that is a shame." He promised Darcy that his insight into Wickycoin was no fluke. These kinds of gains could be made again, and again, and again. But more than this, Wickham wanted Darcy to be an early investor in his company, a "one-stop shop for all things Crypto. We're ahead of the curve, Fitz."

"And what am I going to tell my wife?"

He shrugged his shoulders. "That she looks good in her new dress. I don't know. What do men like you tell their wives?"

"Something happened with you and her sister, Lydia."

"We had a party. It was fun. Nobody got hurt. Then the woke mind virus spread across society and they came for everyone's balls."

"But you sell the world an image of yourself. If we join forces, I amplify that image."

"I don't break the law, Fitz. But if getting rich isn't something that interests you, perhaps I'll need to look elsewhere."

"Tell me something," he said, taking Wickham's wrist. "Did anything happen with my sister?"

"*Your* sister? Come on, Fitz. She was like family to me."

Darcy sighed. Perhaps Wickham did have some shame.

"If this whole thing works out, I could build Elizabeth a foundation," he said, and he said it again as he drove home, and later to her face. He spoke about it all night, and for the rest of the week. It became his obsession. And while in the months that followed he spent his days with Wickham, and their new associates, his evenings were spent dreaming of this foundation. What would they do? Who would they hire? What would the building look like? How many lives could they touch?

Within a year his portfolio had grown tenfold, something even his own father could not have dreamed of. Elizabeth had drawn up detailed proposals for the Bennet-Darcy Foundation, which would work to reconnect marginalized youth with the natural environment, and fund the education of those who wanted to work in environmental careers. It was only weeks away from launching when Darcy woke in the grey pre-dawn light to a call from Wickham.

"They're pulling funds," the voice on the other end of the line informed him.

Darcy hung up and went online. The news was just breaking. Wickham—a reporter for the Wallstreet Journal claimed—had found a way to siphon money directly from his customers' accounts.

Two hours later the men sat opposite one another in the empty boardroom. The AC the only sound in the office—they'd told everyone to stay home.

"Of course it's not true, Fitz," Wickham said, as he paced up and down in front of the enormous windows looking out over the city. "But we need you to make a statement."

"Elizabeth doesn't know that this... that *your* firm is where most of my money is tied up."

"She's going to find out one way or another, Fitz. Better from you."

"Look at me, Wickham." He grabbed the other by the forearm to keep him still. "If I make this statement, I'm using my name, my *father's* name, to stop a bank run on your fund. The Darcy name has power, but if you're lying to me, this will be the end of that name. Look me in the eye, George. Tell me you didn't do this."

"I didn't do it," the other said, gazing deep into Darcy's eyes. "It's just a panic, and regular people will get hurt. You can help those people; save their money."

So that afternoon he made a statement, and by the evening the rush to draw funds had stopped. But when he opened the door to his own apartment he heard Elizabeth's gentle sobbing. In the half light he saw her on the couch, a glass of wine in her hand.

"How?" was all she said, intense pain in her voice. "Why?"

"Where did you think the money was coming from?"

"So it's my fault for believing you?"

"I never said I wasn't working with him."

"Fitz! That man abused my sister," she said, getting to her feet, pointing with her wine glass hand to the television set, which was turned off.

"He said he didn't."

She bit her lip. "And you believed him? Evidently—from your viral testimony today—you also believed him when he said he wasn't stealing money from his customers."

"I did. And I do."

"Fitz," she said, and then again, just "why?"

"He's shady, yes. He's not a criminal."

"Why?" she gazed at him, as if she truly wanted to know, needed to know.

"I wanted us—you—to have your foundation. We still will. This will all pass. It already is passing by. Withdrawals have stopped."

"Yes, because you leveraged your family name to save... Wickham. You only get to do that once. Why?"

"I wanted..."

"To make so much money that you outdid your own father?"

He looked down at his feet. Was it really that simple? What foolish pride.

"You wanted to be your own man?" she said. "But you were the only one who seemed to doubt you were."

"It'll all be fine. This will settle. This will pass."

She finished her wine and left the room.

Of course, it did not pass. In the weeks that followed evidence of Wickham's misdeeds overwhelmed the public until not even his greatest admirers could believe him innocent. When building the trading platforms Wickham had installed a digital backdoor that allowed him to use customer money like it was his own piggybank. Within a month, a company once worth billions was worth less than zero. Darcy had lost his house, and much, much worse, his beloved Elizabeth. Now he slept in his car, ate gas station food, and used truck stops for showers.

So why, on this unseasonably cool evening, as the fog lay low on the roads, did he make his way up Mulholland Drive to the house where Wickham was staying as he awaited his trial? Why did he have a gun in the seat next to him? And why—for perhaps only the third time in his life—was he drinking straight from a bottle of whisky?

It's not as if his killing Wickham would bring Elizabeth home. Nor would it return the money to the orphans and widows whose funds had been plundered, or bring back from the grave the investors who'd thrown themselves from windows. But perhaps it would do something to restore to Darcy a sense of honor. So he reasoned as he took another swig from his whisky bottle, steering clumsily around a tight corner. It was his name, his family name that had restored a moment's calm, restored the public's faith in Wickham, if just for a week. And it was that week that counted. For many, that would have been the moment to escape. Oh, he'd done worse than irreparable damage to his family name.

Now if he couldn't be good, at least he could be infamous. Infamous was so much better than foolish, pathetic, or weak. So he reasoned as he parked his car, slipped his gun into his pocket and walked up the stairs to Wickham's door, ducking beneath the bougainvillea plant that curled above the entrance.

The door was unlocked. The light was off. He pulled on his gloves, turned on the light, and there was Wickham, sitting on a chair, facing the door, as if waiting for him.

"George," he said, voice slurred. "Are you waiting for me to kill you? Do you have one, single, ounce of shame? Is that it?"

Wickham said not word. His chin, Darcy now saw, was almost touching his chest.

"Are you drunk, Wickham?" He took his gun out. "I'm going to kill you, and I'm not going to hide it. I want the world to know that real justice has been delivered. It's not personal revenge. No... Wickham!" He shouted.

Dropping to his knees, he moved his face close to the other man's. "George?" He slapped the man across his face, and only then did he realize: Wickham was dead.

Darcy senior had left his son an emergency fund, a backup parachute in case all his other plans failed. Darcy's pride had meant that for the past months he'd rather live in his car, than touch that money, but now, at the sight of Wickham, something in him shifted, and he felt he owed himself grace.

"I'd been willing to do it," he said, as he checked into a hotel downtown.

It felt so good to have a shower, in a private bathroom, not surrounded by truckdrivers and the smell of smoke-stained clothes. He slipped into bed, after taking a final swig from the whisky bottle. Perhaps I'll know what to do with my life when I wake up, he thought, as he turned off the bedside light. I have that million dollars. That's enough to start a new life.

But he was woken to the sound of the door rattling. A woman came in, moving in a way he knew, a walk he knew.

"My Elizabeth," he said, sitting up in bed.

She turned the light on.

"You came back to me. You found me here. How?" He looked at her now, as she stood very still, watching him. "You died your hair?" he said, trying to focus his eyes. Somehow the sleep had made him even drunker.

"I've always had red hair," she said, sitting on the edge of the bed next to him.

"Lydia?" he said, his head spinning like a top.

"I appreciate that you were willing to shoot him. Women prefer poison," she said. "That's how we like to kill."

"You... killed Wickham?"

"I'd been planning to do it for five years, but I figured now the list of suspects would be as long as it'll ever be. At least that will buy me some time."

"Time," he said. "Yes. You actually killed Wickham. I..."

"He did worse to me. I was only sixteen."

"It's true then, huh?"

"Yes."

"That fucking guy." He looked at her. "Where's Elizabeth?"

"I don't know."

"Will she... ever see me again?"

"I don't know. She's very stubborn. Fitz, I may have some time, but they will find me. In the end. I don't know how, but they will."

"Possibly."

"I need to get out of the country. I know you don't have any money left, but maybe you still have connections, or even ideas."

"I do... have... a little bit of money left. I'll help you get out the country. You can have what I have. You did what I should have done."

It took him a full day to sober up, and a week to get all the money into Lydia's hands. He told her not to let even him know where she was going.

"I won't forget this, Fitz," Lydia said, as they stood waiting for her taxi to the airport.

"You did what I should I have done," he said. "We each get to live more. Let's hope our second lives are better."

They hugged. She hopped into the taxi and was gone.

Months passed before he saw Elizabeth again. It happened one afternoon only a mile from where they'd once lived. He was going in to the coffeeshop as she was coming out.

"Elizabeth," he said.

"Fitz?" She stopped and stared at him. In her hand she held a folder.

"Can we... talk?"

She looked at her watch. "I have a meeting in thirty minutes, but, yes, I guess, we can."

They found a table in the corner of the shop.

"How have you been?" she asked.

"I've had better years," he said.

She looked about the room. "So, there'll be no trial for Wickham after all."

"He did the honorable thing."

"Taking his life?"

"As the papers said."

"I heard from Lydia." She lowered her voice to a whisper. "I know what you did for her."

"It was the least I could do. I owed her more than that."

"That's true," she said. "You did. But that was the right thing to do, and you did it." She touched his forearm gently. "I'll remember that. Even if I'll struggle to forget everything else."

He sucked back tears. "Thank you."

"I must go now, Fitz. I have a meeting."

"Elizabeth," he said, as she stood up. "Maybe one day... one day we could have... I don't know, donuts together?"

She smiled, and looked down at the floor. "We'll see, Fitz. Maybe donuts."

He could not breath as she walked across the room, waiting to see if she'd pause. And she did, in the door, she paused. She turned and looked at him, and he saw the smile on the face that would always be the most beautiful in the world. And then she turned again. And then she was gone.

The End

Michael Rands is the author of the novels *The Chapel St. Perilous* and *Praise Routine Number Four*, co-author of the economic satire *The Yamaguchi Manuscripts*, and *Kamikaze Economics* (a story of modern Japan). He's co-author of the humorous dictionary *Stay Away from Mthatha*. He co-created the audio drama *The Crystal Set* and co-hosted the podcast *Detours Ahead*. In South Africa he worked in television as a writer, director and producer. He taught English in Japan. He holds an MFA from Louisiana State University, and currently teaches English and Creative Writing at the college level. He is the co-founder of Bayou Wolf Press. He lives with his wife, son, and labrador, in Alabama. His new novel, *When the Witch Calls*, comes out in October 2024.

Facebook: https://www.facebook.com/michael.rands.14
Twitter: https://twitter.com/mikerands
Instagram: https://www.instagram.com/michaelrands/?hl=en
Blog: https://medium.com/@notmikerands

NEW YEAR, NEW PROBLEMS

BY LINNÉ ELIZABETH

Liam woke to a sharp jostling. Growling into his pillow, he threw out an arm, hoping to knock over whoever was trying to wake him up at this ungodly hour. Didn't they know New Year's was the one day it's acceptable to sleep in? Especially after babysitting rowdy young adults at the biggest party of the year.

"Wake up, mate." The melodic British accent meant it was Charlie.

Liam considered murdering his best friend but rolled over to face the wall instead. Killing was messy and took too much effort.

"Get up. The crest is gone."

Liam shot up, scrambling to untangle himself from the soft, warm sheets. The shout he intended escaped as a muffled: "What?" He scrubbed a hand over his face; the stubble on his chin pricked his palms, making him more alert. "How long?"

Charlie stood at the edge of Liam's king-sized bed, wringing his hands. With a furrowed brow, he looked to the bedroom door for answers.

Through the slightly ajar door, Liam saw a series of shadows that he guessed were The Pemberley security team. Bunch of cowards. They sent Charlie to do the dirty work.

A deep, distorted voice called, "Sometime between 3 and 5 am."

Liam exhaled and twisted his body to the edge of the bed, wincing as his bare feet rested on the icy wood floor. "Get in here, Fitz."

Fitz pushed his bear-like frame through the door but averted eye contact with Liam. Shoving off the bed, Liam exhaled and paced in front of his cousin and friend while they stood like sentinels.

Liam ran a hand through his midnight-black hair. "Only management and you lot know about that room." He conveniently left off that Georgiana knew about it, too. Their lessons about the family business were in the early stages, and she wouldn't betray him. Neither would the two men in front of him.

Fitz nodded once and placed his meaty hands in front of his body, creating a barrier from Liam's unpredictable mood before volunteering more information. "At 3:30 am, the video feed showed a hooded figure near the lobby door."

A person in a hood loitering by a secret door disguised as a wall during the year's biggest party. That fact alone should have tipped off security. "How many of the team were drunk?"

Charlie cleared his throat.

Liam shook his head. "Don't answer that." His mind jumped from one scenario to another faster than he could process. "We doubled security for this. And new hires were all paired with senior staff."

Fitz nodded again.

Liam threw his hands in the air but kept his voice calm. "And no one saw anything?"

The bedroom door creaked. A large-nosed, pale-faced new hire peeked into their informal meeting. His voice was barely above a whisper. "If I may, sir?"

Charlie approached the door, hand extended, to shut out the headache in the form of a person wanting to "help." The voice piped up louder. "I saw something of note."

Charlie paused and looked at Liam for confirmation to let him in. Liam nodded, resigned to listen to any information that would recover his great-grandfather's crest.

The man slid through the small opening, stopped in Charlie's shadow, and adjusted his vest. He was one piece shy of a three-piece suit and still far too put together for New Year's morning. Tawny, greasy hair fell into his almond eyes as he scanned the room. Crease lines left craggy marks on his cheeks that made him look forty when Liam guessed he was actually in his twenties.

Fitz offered an introduction. "This is Collins. We picked him up for security a couple days ago when Stewart got sick."

"Fill us in, Collins."

At Liam's command, the small man swallowed hard, bowed once like he was addressing royalty, and launched into his account. "I happened to be monitoring the dance floor and noticed an anomaly. A rather petite figure slipped into a secret door. I was about to notify my supervisor, but a lovely woman–Charlotte, was her name, yes. She entranced me with a conversation about her Funko Pop collection. She was telling me about her Harry Potter collectibles…"

With each ridiculous word Collins uttered, Liam's frustration mounted. He exhaled like a valve releasing pressure so he wouldn't toss Collins headfirst out the window. Charlie coughed and shook his head at Collins.

He bowed again. "Yes. Right. I returned to my post just in time to witness the same figure slipping out of that secret door. Based on height and shape, I believe we are looking for a female."

The three men stood stone-faced. Collins's tightlipped smile pulled down into a frown.

"Is that all you saw?" Charlie prodded.

"No. No, indeed. I do consider myself an expert of the female form…"

Fitz snickered.

Collins's frown deepened, but he continued, "This particular form was one I recognized." He paused.

Liam stood, arms crossed over his broad chest, not wanting to voice the question that would satisfy Collins's desperate bid for affirmation.

Unable to withhold his knowledge, Collins shouted, "Well, it was Izzy Bennet, obviously!"

Liam had memorized every name permitted to enter his club, and Izzy Bennett was not one of them. "Who's she?"

Charlie's cheeks flushed, and he looked at his black Converse high tops. "Eh, she's, uh, one of the Bennet sisters."

Liam locked eyes with Charlie. "There was more than one in the club last night?"

Fitz nodded. "There's five sisters total. Three are legal. Charlie here has eyes for Jane." Fitz batted his long eyelashes at Charlie.

Charlie's cheeks flared red to match Fitz's hair. "Shut up, Fitz. It's not like you've never added people on the list before."

Fitz's face drained of color. He rushed to turn the spotlight back to Charlie. "Anyway. It's how Jane got on the list with a plus one. Izzy had to be the plus."

Charlie glanced at Liam with the same expression he had when they were ten and the cook caught them stealing rolls from the cooling rack. He slouched, physically showing his contrition. "I met her yesterday. They just moved in down the street. You were busy with setup, so I added her to the list. I didn't think it would be a problem."

Unsure what to make of an inept security hire and a best friend being led by his …*heart*, Liam pursed his lips. New year, same problems. "Fitz, cue up the security feed and search for this Izzy Bennett. Charlie grab us coffee. I'll meet you two in the office."

Charlie and Fitz jostled each other in a competition to make it out of the room first. The door slammed shut behind them.

"Okay, Google, open the blinds." The thick black blinds retracted to reveal a trickle, then a flood of sunlight. Liam rubbed his temples and did a mental review of last night. He hadn't been drinking because *someone* had to be alert. Yet, he failed to notice a thief leaving The Pemberley with its most treasured item.

For decades his family had operated the widely known, yet best kept, secret in all of Lambton: The Pemberley—a club so exclusive, it remained the most sought-after membership for notable young adults throughout the country. Liam expected the competition to pilfer staff, undercut the annual membership fee, or blackmail him, but stealing The Pemberley Crest was more than a petty business maneuver; it was personal.

As a teenager, Liam's father had first led him through the secret door into the lobby. Floor-to-ceiling mahogany shelves displayed Darcy family achievements from years past. Not a single trophy or medal shined as bright as the 30-centimeter basswood circle hanging at eye level on the wall in front of him. The facade of the crest displayed a detailed carving. A knight's helm sat on a bed of ivy, which spilled halfway down a shield etched in cinquefoils and crosses. It was a rendering of the Darcy family's coat of arms. Liam's fingers had itched to reach out and trace the divots in the wood.

His father placed a hand on his shoulder. "Amazing, isn't it? Your great-grandfather carved this and nailed it here before the grand opening of The Pemberley. It's a reminder of how far we've come. Someday you'll be in charge of this club. It's past, present, and future. What kind of legacy do you want, Fitzwilliam Darcy?"

His legacy wouldn't be to watch the club's downfall. He pulled a pair of dark-washed jeans from the wardrobe and slipped into them.

A light knock sounded at the door. What fresh hell waited for him now? "Yeah?"

A tinkling soprano responded. "Can I come in?"

Liam pulled his door open to greet a head full of dark curls on top of a waif-like form. He smiled, extending a hand to welcome Georgiana into the room. "What's up, Georgie?"

She wrinkled her nose at the nickname. Liam couldn't hide his chuckle. Her annoyed expression lightened the weight of what promised to be an exhausting day. "Some friends are shopping today. Can I go with them?"

Liam quirked an eyebrow. "Who are they? Where will you be? How long will you be gone? Who's driving? Is your cell phone charged?"

She sighed and rolled her eyes at the protective big brother routine. "It's Anne and some of her friends. We're going to Palisade Point. We'll be there between three and five. Aunt Katherine lent us her town car. Swen is driving. And always." She pushed her phone into his face so he could confirm the full charge.

Liam nodded and rubbed her head. She batted his hand away and tried to smooth down the wild curls. "All right. Home by five. I'll check in on you." He held up his phone to display her location. It was a threat wrapped as a promise.

"Yeah, yeah." She rolled her eyes again. "Um, can I also get some money?"

Liam smirked. "For what?"

She shrugged. "For food." Liam stared at her, waiting for her to break. She never could lie, which, as her legal guardian, he appreciated. "Fine. Food and a manicure."

He smiled and walked over to his nightstand. He pressed his thumb to the pad of the drawer and pulled out fifty dollars. "Food and a manicure." He passed her the money.

She rolled it in her palm. Her fingers were bare of jewelry, most notably their mother's intricately twined, pavé diamond-studded white gold band. It had been on her thumb since he gifted it to her on Christmas.

"Where's mum's ring?"

Glancing down, she frowned at her bare hand, then pulled a chain out from her turtleneck. The delicate band dangled from the ancient silver chain. "It kept slipping off. I put it on this chain so I didn't lose it."

He nodded, taking note that a sturdier chain would be a good present for her next birthday. Pacing himself with presents was the most difficult part of being her guardian. "Good call."

"Did you know Anne has one too? I guess Grandpa made family rings for Mum and Aunt Katherine. Anne convinced Aunt Katherine to give hers up so we can have heirloom best cousin rings." She smiled and tucked the band under her sweater before pressing up on her toes to kiss his cheek. "Thanks for the money. I'll see you at five."

Liam watched her skip out the door, hoping he would be home by five, too.

Liam's phone buzzed in his back pocket. He tossed his green Henley over his shoulder and pulled it out, shuddering as his exposed skin prickled with the cool air in the atrium.

Fitz: Check out this clip.

Pressing his thumb to the phone, he unlocked it and waited for the file to open. The manicured square lawn in the front of The Pemberley appeared. In muted colors, a slender figure in an over-sized dark hoodie faced an athletic guy who stood a couple of inches taller. Dark hoodie's position hid her or his face, but the doofus with a charming smile and California surfer hair stood in full view.

Wickham.

Liam hurried down the grand staircase, pulling on his shirt with a force that might tear a seam. His head popped out the neck hole in time to catch himself from running into Caroline. Her blue bonnet eyes roamed his body like it was breakfast and she was starving. "Fitzwilliam Darcy, why the rush?"

Her prim pink lips pulled up into a smirk as she draped her long sleek platinum hair over one shoulder. She closed the distance between them, but remained one stair lower, giving him the perfect view down her tight V-neck sweater.

Eyes locked on hers, he refused to take the bait. "Business." He sidestepped her and sped down the remaining stairs.

"That's a shame."

He paused on the tile floor but didn't turn around. Caroline was relentless, and although it grated on him, he respected the hustle. He shot her down; she bounced back, but he lacked patience for this dance today.

"I was just coming to see if you'd go snowboarding with me." The clack of her heels sounded behind him in a steady rhythm.

"You don't snowboard."

"I can learn with the right teacher."

Pressure built in his temples. He pinched the bridge of his nose. "Not today." He took measured steps, forcing himself not to sprint away from what was sure to become a battle.

She huffed. "Sure, run off to hunt for Izzy Bennet." She emphasized the name like it was a disease.

He turned sharply and knocked into Caroline's bony shoulder. She tilted, but he gripped her forearms to keep her upright.

"My hero." She leaned into him, but he dropped his hands, forcing her to lean back to keep her balance.

He stepped back to place more space between them. She puffed out her bottom lip in a pout that made her look like a grouper he'd seen while scuba diving in the Bahamas last spring.

A wealth of information flowed through Caroline. Hope chipped at his desire to run away. Perhaps she knew something, anything, that could end his predicament. "What do you know about Izzy?"

She scrutinized her French manicure, then gazed at Liam through thick dark eyelashes. "Nothing, really. Just that Charles said she had something to do with a missing crest."

Liam made an internal note to lay into *Charles* for over-sharing with Caroline. He certainly did not intend to confide in Caroline, but she knew something. If he had to feign interest in this conversation to get what he wanted, he could engage a little longer. "I don't know why she'd take the crest. I mean, I don't even know her."

Caroline scoffed. "That's funny."

Liam narrowed his eyes. "What's funny?"

"That you don't know her, silly."

He shrugged. "I don't."

"Well, I guess that's partly true. But you can't deny you two have a certain chemistry."

The pressure in his head ballooned outward. A migraine was brewing, and Caroline was the reason. She turned her head to the side, evaluating him with a hawk like intensity. "You don't remember?" She shook her head, a motion that screamed he was an idiot to not recall the wildly impressive Izzy Bennett. "It must have been a bad kiss."

Liam's chest warmed at the memory of a curvy brunette pushing him against the wainscot wall. "Just go with it," she said before pressing her soft lips against his. He went rigid as stone, but she'd gro wn bolder and deepened the kiss. He placed his hands on her hips and pulled her closer. Much to his disappointment, a slender and striking blonde had pulled her off of him.

He cleared his throat. "I stand corrected. Thanks for putting a name to the lips." Caroline's smirk disappeared. He couldn't miss the opportunity to annoy her. "It was . . . quite memorable."

Caroline dropped her hands to her sides and tightened her fists. Grinning with satisfaction, he turned his back to her and moved two steps closer to his escape before she called out to him once more.

"Seems like she was the perfect distraction."

He stopped and turned to face her, hating the fact that her cryptic comments held power over him. "What do you mean, distraction?"

Caroline brushed at the billowing sleeve of her floral sweater and shrugged like she didn't have a care in the world. "Just that the most troublesome part of stealing from The Pemberley would be distracting you."

He closed the distance between them and towered over her. To her credit, she didn't flinch. "Caroline, if you know anything about the missing crest, speak now."

Her eyes sparkled with amusement. "I saw Wickham last night." She paraded around him, dragging a finger from his chest to his shoulder and over his back as she strutted toward the door. "And Wickham always knows how to play to your weaknesses." She emphasized the final "s" like the hiss of a snake. Her heels clapped on the tiles and her voice receded. "Rain check on the snowboarding lesson, Liam. You seem a bit too distracted." The front door slammed.

Wickham knew where the crest hung. They'd both worked at The Pemberley behind the scenes in high school and then longer during college. Being red-listed barred him from entering the club, but no one would suspect a beautiful outsider. Especially one with such clever eyes.

Liam took a deep breath and pulled out his phone. "Okay Google: Text Fitz."

"What's the message?"

"Get me Izzy Bennet's address."

Fifteen minutes later, Liam stood on the stoop of an updated brownstone. The building exuded an old-world charm against the updated properties on the street. Ivy twisted up the red-brick facade. Liam studied the intricate patterns, impressed that it could survive in a concrete-dominated neighborhood.

He often wondered the same thing about himself. How was he flourishing in this suffocating concrete jungle when he'd rather be elbow-deep in glasshouse dirt at his country estate?

The door swished open, and the curvy brunette almost stepped into him. Izzy Bennet's intelligent dark eyes went wide as the full moon, and a gasp escaped the lips that mere hours ago pressed against his. He froze, momentarily lost in the depth of her coffee-colored irises infused with a burst of gold around the pupil. She narrowed those very eyes as shock of finding a man outside her door dissolved into distrust. Folding her arms across her chest, she assumed a defensive stance. "We aren't interested in whatever you'."

The venom in her tone jolted Liam from his daze. "Are you Izzy Bennet?"

"Elizabeth." With a scornful gaze, she assessed him as if he were garbage. Liam shifted his weight, uncomfortable under her scrutiny. No one dared challenge him this way. Her lips turned up at the corner with a knowing grin, almost as if she could sense his discomfort. "Only my friends call me Izzy."

It was a power play. One he admired, and one he could challenge. He rolled his shoulders back and his lips turned up at the corners. She didn't recognize him as the man she kissed. "As I said, Izzy —"

"Elizabeth," she corrected him again.

He smiled, revealing all his teeth in what Georgiana deemed his Prince Charming smile. "But you said your friends call you Izzy."

She cocked her head to the side, her face tight with impatience. "Yes, I did."

Liam waited for her to continue, but she remained silent. He leaned back on the wrought-iron gate that framed the concrete stoop. "Your lips on mine last night suggests we're more than strangers. So, what shall I call you?"

Her cheeks tinged pink and heightened the golden hue in her eyes. Liam's heart rate spiked. She stepped out of the house, closing the door behind her. And with that, he gained the upper ground.

The sharp edge of her tone melted into something soft and inviting. "Oh! Right. I didn't think I'd see you again. I'm sorry I didn't recognize you. The club was dark. You don't care about that. Look.

There was this guy. He wasn't taking 'no' for an answer. I'm sorry if it made you uncomfortable . . . Or gave you the wrong idea . . . . I just —"

Liam held up a hand for her to stop. While her rambling was endearing, he didn't have time to listen to whatever lies she'd spin. "I am here about the crest."

Her brow furrowed. "Crest? What crest?"

"This doesn't need to be difficult. I won't press charges if you just tell me what happened to The Pemberley Crest." Caroline's accusation crept back into his mind, fueling his desire to know why Izzy Bennet would personally attack someone she didn't even know. "Someone saw you with Wickham. Did he convince you to distract me so he could take it?"

Izzy stood up taller. "I don't know anything about a crest or a Wickham. Beyond a reckless kiss to avoid a creeper, I don't know you. You should leave."

She turned to retreat inside her house, but Liam's frustration flared. He grabbed the door handle to prevent her escape. "That crest is worth more than you will make in a lifetime. It went missing last night, close to the time you locked lips with me. I want it back, Izzy."

She glared at him, picked up her boot, and slammed the heel on his white Achilles sneaker. A hiss escaped his mouth, and he jumped back, stumbling down two steps, but thankfully remained upright while putting all his weight on his left leg.

She leaned over his hunched form. "It's Elizabeth. And I don't owe you an explanation, but the only reason I went to that pretentious club was to drag my fifteen-year-old sister home." Her lip curled in disgust, and she looked down at the black scuff on the otherwise pristine shoe. "You might want to get ice on that. Now get off my porch before I report you for harassment."

The throbbing pain in his foot dulled at the fire in Izzy's eyes and the conviction of her explanation. With his pulse drowning out all sound, Liam realized Caroline's stupid head games not only cost him precious time but also made him look like a limping idiot in front of

Izzy Bennet. Liam snarled at the barb in his pride and winced as he put pressure on his injured foot.

It took Fitz all of five minutes to confirm that Izzy did, in fact, retrieve her younger sister from the club. Well, the video showed the striking blonde (who he learned was Jane) pushing Izzy and pulling a younger girl out the front door around 3:00 am. Izzy was not their culprit. Liam should have gone to Fitz first.

Determined to avoid future false accusations, Liam, Charles, and Fitz locked themselves in the security room to review and re-review the footage from last night. Perched in an executive chair in front of six monitors, Fitz flipped through the recording at a steady pace. Charlie stood behind him, lending a second set of eyes. Liam reclined on the small leather sofa with ice wrapped around his right foot. He replayed the clips of Wickham outside the entrance of The Pemberley with the person wearing the black hoodie, then that same hooded figure slipping into the secret door. Who the hell was it?

Liam exhaled and stared up at the smooth white ceiling. His brash interrogation of Izzy caused him more than a sharp pain in his foot. It filled him with shame. His methodical and even-tempered approach to managing his club flew out the window because of a pair of soft lips. He wasn't any better than Charlie.

If Wickham had something to do with this, Liam needed to keep his focus and hunt down irrefutable evidence. Without it, Wickham would slip out of Liam's grasp back into whatever hole he occupied at the moment.

Charlie made a sharp inhale. "Oh, no way."

Liam peeled himself off the couch and limped over to the screens. It was a 4k version of the clip he'd been replaying for the past hour. The figure in the hoodie slipped through the hidden door into the lobby.

Liam leaned on the desk to get closer to the screen. "I stood up for this?"

Fitz pushed the video back a couple of frames, froze the image, and zoomed in on the slender hand on the door. Long fingers with pink sparkling nails rested on the door with a thumb wrapped in a diamond-studded white gold band.

The frozen image of his mother's ring punched him in the gut. Charlie clapped a hand on Liam's shoulder. Fitz spun away from the screen and brought his steepled fingers to his lips, waiting for the next move.

Liam hung his head and pushed off the desk. "Right. You two handle the club tonight."

Liam rocked in his favorite chair on the wrap around porch of the mansion their parents built but never fully enjoyed. The frigid January air cut through his cotton jacket and jeans. At 4:57 pm, the crunch of gravel signaled an approaching car. Peels of high-pitched laughter floated from the driveway. He pushed off the chair and stood to his full height.

Georgiana and Anne sidled up the sidewalk arm-in-arm, jabbering back and forth, almost tripping over each other with fits of giggles. It was good to see Anne so energized. She'd spent so much of her childhood in a hospital with some illness or other. And Georgiana was happiest with her partner in crime. Disappointment weighed on his heart. He really hoped Georgiana could explain her involvement with an actual crime.

The giggling stopped. Anne's voice broke the silence. "Liam?"

He greeted her in a monotone voice he reserved for business. "Hey, Anne. Thanks for bringing Georgiana home. If you don't mind, I need to speak with my sister." Liam tried to force a smile, but his lips felt heavy as lead.

Anne's smile faltered, and she glanced from Liam to Georgiana. A look of pity flitted across her features. Anne dropped Georgiana's arm and gave her hand a quick squeeze. "I'll see you tomorrow?"

Liam's eyes narrowed on Anne's long pink fingernails and a thumb that sparkled in the dying sunlight. *"Did you know Anne has one too? It's like we have heirloom best cousin rings."*

Anne walked back to the black town car idling in the driveway.

"Wait!" Georgiana and Anne both jumped at the force of Liam's voice.

Anne froze and turned with innocent eyes so wide, Liam could see the white around her irises. She searched around her for a threat. "What? What's wrong?"

Liam stalked toward her and grabbed her right hand. There was the ring that mirrored Georgiana's. Anne pulled her hand from his; her soft eyes flashed granite hard before she dissolved into a teary-eyed mess. Georgianna's eyes creased with concern as she placed a hand on Anne's trembling shoulder.

For the first time in two hours, he took a full breath. Tension melted from his jaw all the way to his injured foot, and Liam trained his eyes on Anne. She sniffled. He narrowed his glare. Years of side-stepping Caroline's advances had honed Liam's ability to recognize emotional manipulation. Anne was a textbook case.

From his peripheral Georgiana quirked her eyebrow. Her expression practically screamed, what's wrong with you?

He didn't have time to fill her in. "Georgiana, I'll meet you inside."

"But --" Liam kept his face neutral and nodded once in the direction of their door. Honestly, where did she think she learned silent communication?

Georgianna rubbed Anne's back and gave her a reassuring smile. As she passed Liam, she used her shoulder as a battering ram in his bicep and stalked up the steps.

Message received. They would debrief tonight.

The front door clicked shut behind him

He trained his attention back on Anne. "Turns out, I need to speak to *you*."

Anne slouched, making herself appear smaller. Liam's heavy disappointment guttered any sympathy for the role she was attempting to play. "Why did you take the crest, Anne?"

Her thin lips pulled into a feral smile that transformed her features from pathetic to sinister. "Took you long enough." She swiped at the false tears. "I'll be the one speaking. *You* will listen."

The End

*** *"New Year, New Problems" was written with the intent to be a standalone short story, but the cliff hanger is killing Linné. So, keep an eye out for more with Liam and Izzy.*

Linné Elizabeth is an English instructor at Utah Tech University, a freelance content writer, and an award-winning author. When she's not devouring chocolate while nose-deep in a book, you can find her playing in the russet desert of southern Utah with her four incredible - sometimes feral - kids and her handsome husband. Check her out on Instagram: @library4one or on Facebook: @linneelizabeth

AUTHOR LINKS
　　Website: https://sites.google.com/asu.edu/linnemarshportfolio/home

Instagram: @Library4One https://www.linkedin.com/in/linneelizabethmarsh/

LinkedIn: https://www.linkedin.com/in/linneelizabethmarsh/

Facebook: https://www.facebook.com/LinneElizabeth

Blog: https://wordpress.com/view/linneelizabeth.wordpress.com

DETECTIVE WOODHOUSE AND THE GALLERY OF FORGERY

BY EMMA DALGETY

The dainty bell hanging on the door of Ford's Coffee jangled ferociously as Miss Gina Bates rushed inside.

Emma jerked in her seat. Gina Bates in one of her whirlwind moods was always an unwelcome disturbance to the coffeehouse peace.

"Oh, the news!" Miss Bates shrieked. "Have you – have you –" She spun in a full circle as she looked for a target. Her gaze lighted upon Emma; with her eyes peering out from behind thick tortoise-shell glasses and a Cheshire cat grin stretching across her face, Miss Bates descended upon Emma's cozy corner table. "Oh – Emma! Just the young lady I wanted to see!"

Emma shut her laptop with a tad too much force, but put on her best smile for the older woman. "How are you, Miss Bates?"

"Have you heard about the Highbury Museum?" Miss Bates demanded, pulling up a chair for herself; Emma noted the older woman's cheeks were actually red, possibly from running and not just because of her unfortunate neon blush.

"Which one? The natural history museum? The art gallery?" Emma widened her eyes, making herself into a portrait of solicitude and curiosity.

"Oh, it's just dreadful! It's the gallery – the curators have discovered a fake in their collection!"

Emma blinked. Now *this* was an interesting bit of news, far from Miss Bates's general bits of gossip. "Which piece was it?"

"It was *Loveliness Itself* – you know, the piece with the girl and – and the swans –"

"That portrait of a lady with a tree in the background?" Emma corrected, the corners of her mouth turning down slightly.

"That's it! That's the one."

"Surely they aren't discovering it's a fake just now when it's been such a central exhibit for years," Emma objected.

"Well, they aren't! It was taken down for a cleaning last week – and when it was placed back on the wall yesterday, it was fake!"

Emma blinked again. Something about this story didn't sound right, but she couldn't tell whether it was simply because of Miss Bates's presentation, or because the circumstances were so unbelievable. "Why would they have taken it down? *Loveliness Itself* is a part of the permanent display, isn't it?"

Miss Bates nodded. "Don't you see? The painting's been *stolen!* And the thief must have left a fake to cover his tracks." She pushed up her glasses and scooted her chair closer, producing a screech that grated on Emma's ears. "I just don't understand who would take it," she continued, words still tripping out of her mouth. "It's a Highbury favorite – they had no right!"

Emma shrugged. "I don't know how much art thieves care about what we think, Miss Bates."

"Oh, I know, I know... it's just terrible! I've been running around all morning. I have to spread the word – that was Jane's favorite painting, you know!"

Emma gritted her teeth at the mention of her old school rival. "I know she must be devastated," she said sweetly.

"Oh, she is – heartbroken, poor thing. She hasn't posted about it yet, but her email this morning nearly brought me to tears."

Emma stopped herself from scoffing just in time. "That is a real shame." She pulled away from the table and slipped her laptop into her bag. "I do hope Jane recovers from the news."

Miss Bates's grin grew even wider. "It's kind of you to say so, dear. You were always such a good friend to my Jane!"

Emma forced a laugh as Miss Bates stood, gathered her cardigan around herself, and bustled out the door. The laugh ceased as soon as the door's bell settled. Emma turned to the barista, Harriet Smith, who was leaning forward with both elbows on the counter. "Could I get another white mocha, please?"

Harriet giggled and rang one up. "What do you think, Emma?" Her wide brown eyes glowed with an excitement that belied her usual shyness. "That was very mysterious, wasn't it?"

Emma laughed. "Mysterious? You've been listening to those audiobooks again, haven't you?"

Harriet blew out a dramatic sigh as she worked. "How did you know?"

"I know how you are, dear. You want a good intrigue just as much as I do."

"Yes, but I can't ever figure them out. Not like you seem to."

Emma grinned at that. "The plots are difficult, but they aren't too bad once you know what to look for. Some days I wonder that I didn't become a sort of detective or private eye."

Harriet turned to Emma with a cup in hand. "Well, why don't you? You said you don't have much in the way of work this week, do you?"

Emma stared at her for a moment. "What do you mean?"

"Emma Woodhouse, don't tell me you aren't wondering who stole that painting! It was written all over your face – you're dying to know."

Emma was going to argue, but realized Harriet's observation was true. "You know… I do wonder," she admitted, folding her arms and glancing up at the ceiling. "*Loveliness Itself* was one of my favorites. I still remember studying it when I was in high school."

"You also know practically everyone in town, Emma. If there's anyone who could track down the thief, it's you."

Emma nodded thoughtfully. "Maybe so." She couldn't bring herself to deny that the idea was a tempting one. She'd tried her hand at dozens of mystery stories and solved so many novels before the end, hadn't she? And with her knowledge of art from the museum workshops she'd attended in high school, she'd surely be able to spot other forgeries should the need arise.

Besides, everyone said she was clever enough. Why not apply her gifts and do the community a service?

"Why not give it a go?" Harriet held out the coffee to Emma. "And then we can have a little party here whenever you figure out who did it, and – oh! We could even invite the culprit, whoever it is! Plan a delicious setup."

Emma's smile grew wider at Harriet's enthusiasm. A reason to host a party was never unwelcome. But a party that culminated in a triumph and possibly a dramatic exit for the thief? Now *that* was a scheme too delightful to resist.

"I haven't been to the art museum in a while. Perhaps it's time for me to pay it a visit."

Apparently, everybody had been talking about this theft. Highbury's news networks and reliable gossip sources buzzed with speculation. Everybody had their own two cents to contribute. As Emma left the coffee shop and walked to the Highbury Museum of Art, she noticed more than a few locals engaged in the activity of combing through their contact lists and stalking Facebook profiles, possibly gathering their own lists of suspects.

Emma knew the risks of visiting the museum. Anyone could see her visiting and throw her name into the ring of popular suspects to be ripped apart by the gossips. As high as her social standing was, Emma wasn't sure if she trusted it enough for complete diplomatic immunity.

Though the museum sign was flipped to CLOSED, Emma found the glass doors unlocked. She walked in and noticed a congregation of police and museum staff gathered at the opposite end of the atrium. Their voices bounced off the walls and formed an unpleasant tangle of echoes.

She slowly approached the group at the end, peering to see if there were any employees she recognized. She spotted Mr. Elton, one of the curators, wringing his hands and looking as overly distressed as possible. She then noticed another familiar face or two, as well as…

John Knightley? Emma blinked, not completely sure why her nextdoor neighbor and family friend would be in the throng.

Knightley, who stood a good head and shoulders taller than most of the others, spotted her across the atrium and raised an eyebrow. Emma gave a subtle shake of her head. She didn't want to interrupt – only to listen.

"And you noticed the swap yesterday afternoon?" one of the officers asked Mr. Elton.

"I… yes," Mr. Elton said. Emma wrinkled her nose at how his whining tone carried in the live space. "It was brought to our attention by a frequent patron of ours…"

"That frequent patron being me. I noticed the swap yesterday," Knightley interjected. Mr. Elton glared at him as soon as he began speaking. "The theft had to have occurred during its scheduled removal for cleaning, sometime last week. It looked fine to me when I saw it last Tuesday."

"And what prompted you to look so closely at the signature?" one officer asked.

Knightley shrugged. "I was just looking at it. I didn't set out to discover the painting was a forgery."

Emma shook her head.

The officer looked at his associates. "Well, we've got our work cut out for us – we'll need to review all of the security footage from the past week. So we'll take our leave, gentlemen."

"Yes, of course – we'll be in touch," Mr. Elton said with an ingratiating smile on his face. As soon as the officers' backs were turned, he gave Knightley another glare, then departed down another hall.

Emma decided she'd waited long enough and went over to Knightley. "That seemed to go well," she remarked wryly.

Knightley rolled his eyes and started towards the door. "Mr. Elton is upset. I think I've hurt his pride by out-curating him yesterday, and now he has to live with the consequences of that for the time being." He glanced sideways at Emma, his eyes narrowing. "What brings you here? You didn't happen to notice the fake, too, did you?"

"Me? Oh, no – I haven't been here for a few years now. Miss Bates told me what happened, though. I decided I'd like to come see for myself."

Knightley slowed. "Come see the forgery?"

"Of course. And the crime scene, too, if possible."

Knightley gave her a baffled look. "Emma, I don't think that's legal."

"I want to help," Emma insisted, ignoring his excellent point. "The police have their hands full as is – they can't make this case their one responsibility. I don't have any pressing responsibilities this week, so I can focus all of my energy into figuring out who stole *Loveliness Itself.*"

Knightley was quiet for a moment, then burst into laughter. Emma stiffened. "Emma, look..." he regained his composure. "You are clever enough to maybe solve a murder mystery novel before the rest of us do. I'll give you that. But this is a real case; it's not as simple as fiction. And while I was able to spot the forgery, I couldn't hope to guess who swapped that painting over the course of the week. The art thief has a head start on everyone – the painting could be as far off as London now, for all we know."

Emma crossed her arms and jutted out her chin, not even bothering to conceal her displeasure. "I'd like to see the scene for myself, please."

Knightley spluttered. "Emma Woodhouse, did you hear anything I just said?"

"Miss Woodhouse?" Knightley and Emma turned. Mr. Elton was peering out from around the corner. He once again wore his best fake smile, though he seemed to be doing his best to keep Knightley out of his direct line of vision. "Am I hearing correctly? You've come to play detective?" He laughed, folding his arms.

Emma glanced sideways at Mr. Elton. "If you would like my help, I'm willing to give it a go. I've got the connections and research skills for it – and certainly you remember how I used to take art lessons here. I think I could be of some service." Mr. Knightley let out a strangled sort of groan at that and dragged a hand down his face.

"Ah, well with your talents and qualifications, I don't see why we shouldn't let you investigate," Mr. Elton said almost too quickly. "Feel free to come and go as you please – no admission charge. And do feel free to discuss your findings with me at any time – my office door is always open."

Emma's smile faltered a little. "Thank you, Mr. Elton. I'll keep you posted if I find anything out. Have a great day." She turned away and nodded in the direction of the door for Knightley to follow her.

"Do you see why this is a terrible idea on multiple levels, Emma?" Knightley asked as soon as they were out the door. He gave her a wry smile. "You really want to work with Mr. Elton on this hobby case of yours?"

"Of course not. I have no intentions of working with him more than I have to," Emma replied coolly.

Knightley stopped walking. "Why's that?"

"Because Mr. Elton is my first suspect, of course."

"What?" Knightley shook his head. "Elton is... well, Elton. But he isn't a thief, Emma. On what grounds are you basing this accusation?"

"He just seems suspicious to me." Emma smirked. "Besides Knightley, Mr. Elton is the one who organizes these paintings and schedules their rotations. He had the greatest opportunity to swap out the original for a forgery, I think. But that isn't to say I won't gather more suspects. Mr. Elton is the only one who has presented himself to me so far."

Emma opened up her phone and started typing a note, blocking out Knightley and his unwelcome input.

"This..." Knightley sighed and dragged a hand through his hair. "Emma, this is complete foolishness."

Emma put up her phone and gave him her best glare. "Well, we're all entitled to our own opinions, aren't we? I'll leave you to your rather disagreeable one now." With that, she beat a hasty retreat back in the direction of Ford's.

Halfway down the street, however, she paused. She opened her phone and added Knightley's name to her list of suspects as an afterthought. If he had such a strong objection to her involvement in this Highbury mystery, then that was enough to arouse her suspicions.

Though part of her knew it was petty, seeing Knightley's name near the top of her list and imagining his outrage did bring a smile to Emma's face.

The next morning, Emma walked into Ford's only to be greeted not by Harriet's customary welcome, but rather by a cry and a frantic wave from the barista. "Emma! I've been waiting for you!" She beamed at her from across the room.

Emma hustled over to the counter, her heart sinking a little. She recognized Harriet's expression – it was one she usually wore when she took the liberty of making a decision without Emma's input. Such unpredictable decisions usually came with a predictable side of disaster. "What is it?"

Hanna rang up Emma's usual and took her card without asking. "I've been thinking about that mystery of yours and I think I know how I can help. How has it been coming along?"

"Oh, I'm not totally far into the investigation yet. I have a suspect or two, and I plan to do some asking around today. Try to collect some evidence." Emma relaxed a little but not entirely. *Thinking* about how to help was better than Emma had expected. At least Harriet hadn't done anything rash... right?

"Good. Do you think that you'll reasonably solve it soon?"

Emma laughed. "I hope so? It depends on what I find today."

"So... by the end of the week, maybe?" Harriet held out Emma's coffee to her.

"If I find what I'm looking for, then yes."

"Great. Because I took the liberty of booking a night here for the reveal party."

Emma's smile froze on her face. "You – Harriet, you did *what?*"

"It's what's done in all of the good stories, you know!" Harriet laughed, oblivious to the panic that flashed across Emma's features. "Once you solve the mystery, we can meet here with the regulars and the culprit. It'd be an event for Ford's to remember!"

Emma opened her mouth and closed it again, at an uncharacteristic loss for words. "Harriet, I don't think I can guarantee that –"

The bell on the door jangled again like a gunshot. "Welcome to Ford's!" Harriet called, shooting Emma an apologetic glance.

Breathing a sigh, Emma took her drink and retreated to her usual corner, with all the pressure of this new deadline washing over her. The unwelcome dread of social embarrassment sapped all of the delight out of the intrigue for her. Rather than glowing success, Emma now imagined the searing ridicule of the gossips that would follow if she failed publicly.

Unfortunately for Emma, it was Gina Bates who had once again blown through the door like a hurricane. Without even pausing to order a drink, she hustled over to Emma's table. "Just the friend I wanted to see!" she crowed. Emma winced as the woman pulled her bulky phone out of her cardigan pocket. "Just look at Jane's new post! It's not about the painting — I couldn't have expected — How is it we hadn't heard anything — and the size of it —!"

Of what? Her ego? Her crowd of devoted followers? Emma bit her tongue to silence her ugly retorts and put on her best smile. "I haven't checked my phone today..." She was momentarily distracted by Harriet's raised eyebrows and skeptical stare. "What did Jane post?" She asked quickly to smooth over the lie.

"*She's engaged!!*" Miss Bates cried, plenty loud enough for all the morning regulars to hear.

Ford's exploded into a frenzy and pandemonium that Emma was very ill-prepared to handle with grace and decorum. "Let me see!" she demanded over the noise of the other busybodies in the coffee shop, reaching for the phone.

Miss Bates could hardly hold the phone out to Emma, as she was jittering too much for anyone to see the post clearly. But Emma could still make out the focal point of the post: an engagement ring of considerable size and sparkle.

"Goodness!" Emma cried. "Who on earth is she engaged *to?!*" And how much did a ring of that size even *cost?*

"It must have cost a fortune!" Harriet interjected as she leaned fully over the counter to see the picture. Marriages and engagements were her favorite subjects of conversation, and even more compelling than mysteries.

"She's engaged to Frank Churchill! Can you believe it?"

"Wait – the same Frank Churchill who flunked out of college and went off to Weymouth?"

"Emma dearie, no one remembers him that way except you!" Emma spluttered at Miss Bates's comeback. "But you are right! It is Highbury's one and the same Frank Churchill."

Emma blinked. "That's... great news." She smiled in an attempt to hide the shock. "What is he doing now? He must be doing very well for himself since he moved."

"I'm not sure – last time Jane mentioned him in our emails, he was looking into cryptocurrency. Looks like it worked out very well for him.”

“No kidding,” Emma muttered, shaking her head and passing the phone back to Miss Bates. “Well, congratulations to them both. I’m sure they will be perfect for one another.”

“So kind of you to say so, dear! I’ll catch you all later – I think I must start planning for this wedding as soon as possible!” Miss Bates whirled out of the coffee shop once more, leaving a hurricane of confusion in her wake.

Harriet glanced at Emma and opened her mouth to say something, but Emma held up a hand and stopped her. “I think I need to go talk to Knightley. I’ll be back,” she said, rushing out the door just as urgently as Miss Bates.

Emma’s clomping high heeled boots could be heard from several feet away as she marched up the path to Knightley in Box Hill Gardens. He was sitting on a bench, wholly absorbed in reading a book. “Knightley, did you know about Frank Churchill and Jane Fairfax?” she demanded from a ways off, loud enough to send some of the pigeons scattering.

Knightley jumped, then snapped his book shut. “Hello to you, too,” he said quickly, his brow furrowing. “What about them?”

“They’re engaged now.”

Knightley’s eyebrows shot up at the news. “Are they really?” He stood up and started pacing back and forth. “That’s odd. Didn’t he flunk out of college?”

“Knightley, you’re the only one who remembers him that way. But yes.”

Knightley’s brow furrowed. “That is… odd. How on earth did he get the money? Why would Jane accept him?”

“Knightley! It’s not our place to ask such a thing. But I did hear from Miss Bates that he was dabbling in cryptocurrency, so that might answer your question.”

Knightley let out a bark of laughter. “I’m not sure it does. In my understanding, cryptocurrency requires a level of competency to be successful – a level that I know Frank lacks."

Emma huffed. "What are you suggesting?"

Knightley looked up at her and stopped pacing. "You wouldn't have mentioned this to me if you didn't find it strange yourself. I'm wondering if he found an easy way to fund his unambitious lifestyle. Has he posted anything?"

"I mentioned it to you because I found the timing strange – not because I want to accuse Frank Churchill of anything," Emma objected, wrinkling her nose.

"Oh? Is that true?" Knightley smiled a little. "I wondered if you would want to add him to your suspects list. Is the surprise engagement suspicious enough to earn him a spot? How could he have gotten the money so quickly?"

Emma's mouth fell open, and she glared at him. "John Knightley, you're just being ridiculous! Frank has been in Weymouth for the past several years, aside from the occasional visit to family here in Highbury."

"And who's to say that he didn't pay a visit to the art museum recently?"

"He would have had his work cut out for him escaping detection – everyone would have recognized him! We'd all be talking about it if he set foot anywhere in town."

Knightley shrugged, his smile growing wider. "Maybe, maybe not. But I thought you of all people might be pleased to have such a wonderful suspect to investigate."

"I don't need your ridicule!" Emma snapped. "You're just mocking me now. Why are you so against me trying to figure this out?"

"I'm not against you, Emma," Knightley said with an air of surprise. "I just know your tendency to get into situations way over your head. As a friend, am I allowed to notice and say something, or at least offer my thoughts? I'm not against helping you, you know; I actually want to help."

"Oh, really? Why should I believe you?"

Knightley laughed. "Are you serious?"

"Completely. You weren't particularly helpful to the police except in pointing out the forgery. I don't see you offering your services to help them, or me for that matter. You've been against the investigation from the start."

"Well, that would be because I'm refraining from pointless speculation, Emma," Knightley objected in a mild tone. "I'd rather let the experts and professionals handle it and observe from the sidelines."

"Well, you consider yourself such an expert in all things having to do with *Loveliness Itself,*" Emma retorted, glaring at Knightley. "How did you know to check the signature? Were you *expecting* to find it forged?"

"No, Emma," Knightley said with a chuckle that grated on Emma's nerves. "I stop by the painting all the time and wanted to take a closer look after its supposed 'cleaning' or restoration. That was when I noticed the extra loop in the font." His smile faded, and he looked at her more closely. "You don't mean to tell me that you put me on your suspect list." He looked as if he were trying his best to keep in his laughter.

Emma let out a growl of frustration. "Call it my "suspicious persons" list. I've barely been on this case for a day. But as your friend, am I not allowed to notice when you're acting strangely? Because you *have* been off ever since reporting that painting."

Knightley looked up at the sky for a moment. "You're certainly welcome to think that. Though I think I've been as consistent as ever."

"As consistently *insufferable* as ever, maybe!"

Before he could respond, Knightley's phone buzzed, displaying a text from Mr. Elton. "Oh, look – a development for you." He showed her the screen. "This man doesn't have your contact information and luckily has no idea how to use social media to reach you. So I've been getting messages to pass along to you."

"Seriously?" Emma asked, unimpressed. "What is he saying now?"

"Let's see – oh!" He opened up the message, his brow furrowing once more in an intense expression. "I don't understand. Elton says that the painting has been switched again."

Emma cocked her head. "What? Does he mean he's discovered another forgery?"

"No. He's saying that the forgery has been replaced with another piece of artwork entirely."

"What? Was that a museum decision?" Emma asked, her frustration forgotten as confusion set in.

"It must have been; I'm not sure. He sent me a picture and... I'm honestly not quite sure what it is I'm looking at."

"Let me see." Emma came alongside him to better see the picture and the message. At the sight of the image, she froze, and felt her breath catch in her throat.

"Emma?" Knightley prompted, glancing at her out of the corner of his eye.

"If this was a museum decision, it's some sort of cruel joke."

"Why? Do you know this painting?"

"Yes. It's – it's one of *mine*."

The remaining few days in the week passed, slipping through Emma's fingers entirely out of her control. Harriet saw no reason for concern; after all, the greatest detectives often had their greatest moments of revelation at the last possible second, just in time to prevent the criminal mastermind from escaping. Emma would solve it – there was no question about it.

Harriet outdid herself with planning the grand reveal, with a networking skill and efficiency that rivaled Emma's own. Through word of mouth with the regulars at Ford's, Harriet easily reached half of Highbury – which Harriet excitedly made a point to tell Emma when she stopped by that morning.

"I still haven't solved it yet, Harriet," Emma said again later that afternoon, catching her reflection in the shiny surface of the counter. Her careful makeup barely masked the dark circles under her eyes. "I have three very unlikely suspects and hardly enough evidence for any of them."

Harriet looked skeptically at her friend as she took the liberty of adding an extra shot of espresso to Emma's third coffee of the day. "You can and you will. I believe in you."

The bell on the door jangled again, and instinctively Emma braced for impact. Mercifully, it was not Miss Bates. "Knightley?" Harriet and Emma both asked, fixing him with equal looks of confusion. Knightley was *not* a Ford's regular.

Knightley nodded to Harriet. "I'm not ordering. Emma, do you have a moment to discuss tonight?"

Emma stared at him blankly. "The party? Are you coming?"

"Of course I am. I was invited. But I think I can help you, if you'll let me."

"Oh, really? You finally offer to help *now?*"

"This is important. I will only say this once, but it appears that you were right – partially."

Emma couldn't help but smirk at that.

Harriet giggled and passed Emma her coffee. "Go – if this is about the case, don't let me stop you two."

Emma and Knightley took a seat at her usual table. "This is about the case?"

"Yes. Emma... I think you're right to suspect Elton," Knightley said, running a hand through his hair. His eyes were troubled. "'I've been thinking ever since the painting got swapped out again. That painting is yours, yes? How exactly did it end up in the museum?"

"It was one of my assignments when I took lessons at the museum," Emma said with a frown. "Someone would have had to retrieve it from storage. I never knew what happened to that painting after our class display was taken down."

"So... someone would have had to remember that display."

"I don't see who would have remembered it. Jane Fairfax was in that class; her painting outshone everyone else's..." Emma trailed off, her brow furrowing.

Knightley raised an eyebrow. "Do you see where I'm headed?"

Emma opened her mouth, then closed it again. "I don't."

"Elton remembered that exhibit and put your painting up there. He could be trying to frame you... or flatter you. He's a strange one. I tried to ask him about it, and he didn't respond to any of my messages."

Emma rested her elbows on the table and hid her face in her hands. "That wasn't what I was thinking."

"Oh. What have you put together now?"

"Nothing." She blew out a sigh. "Knightley... for once, maybe we were both not entirely correct. I think I've succeeded in making a very tangled and interesting web of social gossip. But the truth of this... definitely isn't as simple as fiction."

Knightley chuckled, but his eyes were kind. "That's brave of you to admit. But don't sell yourself short. I think you've been asking the right questions – as many as you possibly could within three days to meet this arbitrary deadline." He cocked his head. "So what are you going to do about tonight? Your party?"

Emma stared up at the ceiling. "It's still on; I can't cancel it so soon. I'll present my thoughts as they are, but I won't claim to have solved anything. I know I haven't."

"Ah. That is brave, too." Knightley stood and gave her a nod. "May I possibly attend, or is it closed to those who aren't Ford regulars?"

Emma laughed. "Come if you must. You're one of my chief suspects, remember?"

At seven, guests began filing into the coffee shop. By 7:30 pm, Emma Woodhouse had a very rapt and silent audience sitting at the various tables, eyes fixed upon her.

Everybody had their own ideas; would Emma's word on the matter have the final say?

"Thank you all for coming." Emma forced confidence and poise into her tone. "I must confess... this case was and is a difficult one. It may not yet be entirely solved."

"But Harriet said you solved it," someone interjected.

"That's not the point," Emma said quickly, lifting her chin. *Don't stop there. Keep moving.* "The point is... The theft of *Loveliness Itself* has hurt us all, hasn't it? When I heard the news, I couldn't imagine who might have done such a thing. As such, I'd like for you all to help me. Let's reach a conclusion together, shall we?"

The audience was quiet. Emma breathed a little sigh of relief and forged ahead.

"Over the course of the past few days, I have identified three possible suspects. When I arrived at the museum on Tuesday, I witnessed a conversation between the police, Mr. Elton, and Mr. Knightley. You all know from the news reports that Knightley was the first to report the discrepancy in the painting's signature. I personally found it strange that Knightley was the first to notice, and immediately suspected that either something prevented Mr. Elton from reporting the theft, or he had a motive to avoid reporting it."

Whispers immediately kicked up at her first accusation; Mr. Elton's acquaintances preparing their defenses, no doubt.

"Then again, the next day I also discovered that Frank Churchill – a name I'm sure you're all familiar with – had recently come into a mysteriously large sum of money. A sum large enough to afford an engagement ring, at least." Emma paused and scanned the room for Miss Bates; she sat at the back of the room with a perplexed expression on her face. Emma internally winced, but continued. "I know that we have not seen him in years, so I did some research of my own, and discovered that he is now an art dealer with a growing reputation. Furthermore, his fiancé, Jane Fairfax –" the murmurs increased to a dull roar at that – "his fiancé is a skilled painter in her own right.

"I am not accusing Jane Fairfax of involvement; she is not one of my primary suspects," Emma continued, unable to take the growing look of dismay on Miss Bates's face. "However, it is possible that Jane's artwork was involved. Yesterday, a painting of my own was placed on the wall without my permission. Several years ago, Jane and I took an art class together at the Highbury Museum. We were assigned the task of painting a work in the same style as *Loveliness Itself*. She painted a near-exact replica at the time... I remember its success all too well." Emma admitted this through a forced smile and gritted teeth. "I have every reason to believe that her painting was in the archives, just like mine. It hung on the wall either upon the discovery of the theft, or as a direct plot between Frank Churchill and Mr. Elton."

"So... who's your third suspect, if it isn't Jane?" Harriet asked, brow furrowed.

Emma looked down at the floor, her face growing warm. "That would be Mr. Knightley." She looked up and spotted him sitting in her usual corner seat. "He attempted to dissuade me from taking on the case. He then suggested the name of Frank Churchill to me. But he would have been just as capable of informing Mr. Elton about the paintings in storage, and perhaps was involved all along in an attempt to misdirect me."

The gathering was rather quiet at that. No one seemed to know what to say; several cast sideways glances at Knightley.

Finally, Knightley chuckled. "So then, Emma, who do you say for certain?"

Emma frowned and waved her hands in defeat. "It must be all three of you; I don't see how it could be only one of you."

Knightley grinned. "Well done, Emma. Allow me to congratulate you. You are not completely wrong."

Emma blinked. That was not the reaction she'd been expecting. "I... how do you know?"

"Simple." Knightley folded his hands and rested them on the table. "The police went through Mr. Elton's correspondence and security cameras and found he had, in fact, been in touch with Frank Churchill to see about finding a buyer for *Loveliness Itself*. I had a feeling that was the case myself, as Mr. Elton was so against the investigation from the start.

"I've been involved with the police since I reported the painting," Knightley confessed. "I have friends there. Your tips and good instincts, Emma, ended up being just what they needed; they now have enough evidence to close the case and are well on their way to recovering the painting." He grinned. "I am not one of the thieves, but you did correctly identify my behavior as being out of the ordinary. So – I say again – well done."

The audience was silent for a moment, but then turned and started applauding Knightley. Emma stared at him and watched until he was swamped in a crowd of curious individuals – with Miss Bates understandably at the head of the army.

"I... I solved it after all," she said quietly.

"You did!" Harriet's eyes danced as she approached Emma. "How does it feel?"

Emma shook her head. "It doesn't feel real." She laughed. "It feels... It feels like a fiction!"

The End

Emma Dalgety grew up in Mobile, Alabama. She received a BA in Music and English from the University of Mobile in 2023. As a musician and a writer, she has performed violin across the Southeast and internationally, finding creative inspiration and filling notebooks with story fragments throughout her travels. When she isn't writing, she is researching interdisciplinary connections in literature as she works towards an MA in English, or teaching music lessons in her private studio.

THE BEGINNING AND THE END

AN AUSTEN UNIVERSITY MYSTERIES SHORT STORY

BY ELIZABETH GILLILAND

"Vanity was **the beginning and the end** of Sir Walter's character; vanity of person and situation." *-Persuasion*

No one had a higher opinion of Professor Walter Elías than Professor Walter Elías, and no one had more concern for maintaining his illustrious reputation.

Nevertheless, if his semesterly course ratings or scores on Rate-MyProfessor were the sole markers of his academic performance, it might have been puzzling to ascertain just how Walter had achieved such a coveted tenured position at a respected private institution such as Austen University, since in both categories he had an average 1.9 score (with 5 being the highest possible ranking). Common complaints included his proclivity for teaching straight from the textbook–often, just reading it out loud to his students in lieu of planning a lesson. His exams were noted to have been recycled without any updating from past years, with some still bearing date stamps from before the turn of the 21st century. He liked to assign impossibly large chunks of reading, along with thorough study guides of said material, that never seemed to actually be read during grading; one student confirmed this by writing out the lyrics to "We Didn't Start the Fire" on a loop for seven pages, only to receive a B. As this was a rather arbitrary grade for Billy Joel's classic song of social upheaval, this led some to speculate that Walter might just be assigning random grades to his students. Just last semester, he'd been reprimanded by the dean for attempting to bully one of his students, Elizabeth Bennet, into dropping his class to curry favor with the president of the university. And he assigned exams on the same day as the university team's football games, which was perhaps the biggest faux pas any professor could commit at a Southern university.

Luckily for Professor Walter Elías, his tenure had not been earned by merit of being an exemplary teacher. As it was a foolish requirement for teachers to actually know how to teach, Walter did not consider himself *lucky* so much as benefiting from the rewards owed to a distinguished individual such as himself. He was an Elías, after all, and came from a long line of Professor Elíases, including his father, uncles, cousins, grandfather, and one great-uncle; and though he had no sons himself, two of his daughters had been accepted as PhD candidates. Luckily, as Ana seemed unlikely to ever marry, the surname would definitely carry on through her. She was only in the history department, though, so when Eliza finally met a match worthy of her, Walter would insist that she also keep the family name. Perhaps her partner would even want to become an Elías, which Walter would graciously allow, so long as they weren't studying anything truly embarrassing like English or theater.

Because of his family connections, it had been easy enough for Walter to get into a good PhD program, helped along no doubt by some well-placed connections of his father's. Nobody liked nepotism until it benefited them, and so Walter liked to rant and rave as much as the next person about privileged students buying their way into the university; it wasn't a double-standard if one was deserving of such handouts and others simply weren't, he reasoned.

Once in a good program, it had been even easier for Walter to find a good lab partner, to whom he could yolk himself to balance out his own lazy mediocrity. And because Walter was not stupid, if also not especially bright, he married this young woman before she could fully realize just how lazy and mediocre he truly was. By the time Anita Peña realized what she'd gotten herself into, it was easier for her to just do most of the work and let Walter take most of the credit. As a white-passing man from a prominent academic family in a predominantly masculine discipline, he *did* open most of the doors, so it was only fair his name should go first on all the papers–or so Anita soon resigned herself.

By the time she died, Walter had been so widely published that he could coast on their shared credentials for the rest of his career if he so chose–and indeed, he did. The steep decline in Walter's research could be attributed to grief; and his reputation was now so well-established that brilliant graduate students were willing to do most of the work if he'd contribute his name to a paper to help put it to the front of the slush pile line at the academic journals. What did it matter if he was a 1.9 teacher if he was a respected, recognized name in his field with an impressive h-index score, after all?

This was such a comforting truth that Walter often checked his h-index score when he was feeling stressed or low. Or when he needed an ego boost. Or when he was bored. Today he was in the first camp, and luckily he was also due for a ratings boost since he'd recently required his graduate students to cite one of his essays in their work before seeking publication in order to receive his endorsement on job applications. Walter had strong-armed an undergraduate into helping him set an alert on his phone for whenever his work was referenced through Google Scholar, and one of his students (he wanted to say Harvey, though in truth, it was actually Neil) had emailed recently that his publication would be out by the end of the week. Any moment now he should get that little ping of recognition that reassured him he was still at the top of his field.

I am a valuable and important person, he reminded himself as he scrolled through social media, trying to distract himself while he waited for that *ping*. He really needed this today, of all days. It had been a difficult month.

Instead, what he got was a *ding*–but not regarding his h-index score, as he had hoped. This alert indicated a new email message–perhaps an update from Harvey 9or whatever his name happened to be)? But as Walter switched windows into his inbox, he saw the 'from' category read 'Unknown.'

More out of boredom than any real intuition or curiosity (two traits rather lacking in the good professor), Walter clicked on the message, frowning as he read its contents. Generally, Walter tried to avoid frowning, as even on a tenured professor's salary, botox to reduce the sign of frown lines was an unattainable luxury. Unfortunately, the contents of this particular email demanded such an expression.

> I know what you did.

As a rule, it is only those with a guilty conscience who would tremble in fear at such a declaration. The reader may draw what deductions they will, but Walter's face paled as he read these words. His hands trembled. His neck broke out in an undignified sweat that could ruin the aesthetic appeal of his ascot tie, a concern that would have usually been at the forefront of his mind.

Yes, Walter's conscience had been extremely guilty as of late. He had been losing sleep. He hadn't entirely lost his appetite, but he hadn't been able to finish his organic smoothie the other morning, and he had a new bar of imported European dark chocolate that had sat unopened in his desk drawer for a week.

It wasn't so much what he had *done* that was making Walter suffer so, but what might happen if anyone were to find out. He had a reputation to uphold. He was one of the university's star academics. He was an Elías. These things didn't simply just disappear over one stupid mistake. And yet... they very well might.

The best thing would probably be to not engage with the email at all. It was probably one of those Phishing scams the faculty were always being warned about, and he would end up losing $5,000 he couldn't afford. All things considered, this outcome made Walter feel hopeful. Maybe it was only someone after his money, not after his reputation.

Still, prudent as it might have been, Walter could not just walk away. He was not especially curious, but he *was* exceedingly vain, and if someone knew something about him, even something incriminating, he had to know what it was.

Who is this?

he emailed back.

The reply came in just a few moments.

> Someone who was out for a drive the night
> of the Croft Gala.

If Walter had been pale before, the reference to the event in question made him positively ghostly. It was a lie, of course; there had been no one else out on the road that night, he'd been absolutely positive about that before he drove away, but the reference to that event couldn't be a coincidence. This person, whoever they were, knew something, somehow.

Still, Walter hoped he could outbluff them. No one had seen anything. No one possibly could have. Whoever it was, they were guessing, that was all, and he wouldn't tell them anything that could give himself away.

Why should I care?

he wrote back.

This time, he received no written message in response, just attachments to several news stories—all of them about the hit-and-run accident that had nearly left Marianne Dashwood dead.

Nearly. That was a bit of an exaggeration. There'd been some broken bones. She'd required a few weeks of physical therapy, but she was going to be fine—and some anonymous benefactor had stepped in to cover her hospital bills. Not Walter, of course. Even if he'd thought of it, which would have required a leap of compassion so great that it would have completely rewritten his character, he wouldn't have been able to afford it.

Plus, Ana was keeping a close eye on their bank statements these days, insisting they scale back and deprive themselves of the things that made life worth living. No wonder he'd been driven to drink a few too many free cocktails at the Croft Gala and hadn't been in possession of his full faculties as he was driving home that night!

And how was he supposed to know that girl—Marnie, he wanted to say—would be walking on the side of the road? He might have even done her a favor by hitting her with his car, sparing her from other worse fates that might have occurred to a young woman, alone, on a quiet road in the middle of the night.

It was doubtful President de Bourgh would see things that way, though. Or the police, for that matter. There were very few things that could lose a professor tenure, but Walter suspected that intoxicated driving and nearly killing (*mildly harming*) a student, then leaving the scene of the crime, might just tip him over the edge.

There was no playing coy with this emailer, whoever it might be. Walter typed furiously, pounding the keypad with more vehemence than it deserved.

What do you want?

What is due to myself,

came the strange, enigmatic reply.

Walter waited several minutes, refreshing a few times, but no other message arrived.

What was *due* to themselves? What an odd turn of phrase. Walter was sure he didn't owe anything to anyone. It was possible there might be a disgruntled student who had disliked a grade they earned on a test, but that was hardly Walter's fault. His TAs did most of his grading. He wondered if it could be that Bennet girl, trying to get revenge on him for nearly failing her in his class...

As quickly as he'd lighted on the idea, however, it passed. Elizabeth Bennet was not the sort who would plot silently. She would write some article and post it all over the Internet, trying to leach out her fifteen minutes of fame. Some people truly had no sense of decorum.

Was the emailer trying to blackmail him? If so, they would be sorely disappointed. And if not, what was their endgame? Walter supposed more messages would follow, since the exchange had been left on only the vaguest of terms. Earlier in the day, he'd been excitedly monitoring his phone, and now every new ping and ding sent his stomach plummeting. He'd already been stressed enough with all the police investigation and news coverage surrounding the hit and run accident, and that had only just begun to die down. Now this? How much suffering did one person have to bear?

Since Walter would always rather suffer in company than alone, he decided to pay a visit to his favorite daughter, Eliza. She wasn't the sort who would comfort him, per se, but her droll snarkiness was a balm to his soul. Of course, she knew nothing about the hit and run accident, since he would never want to diminish the heroic presence he was in her mind; but he could find a vaguer way to vent his frustrations, and she would always come up with the best solutions, like trying out the newest boba tea place or going for a fish pedicure.

And even if he *did* tell her the truth, Eliza wasn't a nagging scold like Ana, who would most definitely tell him it was his moral obligation to turn himself in to the police, and remind him that farming garra ruffa fish was meant to be unethical.

Before stepping into the Science and Engineering Department office, Walter took a moment to compose himself. It wouldn't do to appear frazzled or haggard, not only because it might raise suspicions, but also because he had a reputation to uphold as one of the best-dressed professors in the STEM field. He stopped in the men's bathroom to freshen his breath and make sure his well-coiffed hair was still in place. A moment later, he breezed into the room, smiling at the two receptionists.

"Penelope, Eliza. How are my two favorite student workers on campus?"

Penelope Clay giggled, sitting up straighter and arching out her breasts at Walter's approach. She was not the prettiest girl they could have put at the front desk, but she did have a good sense of humor, always laughing at his little witticisms, as well as a very nice…decolletage, as the French might say. Gossip ran rampant at a small school like Austen University, so he knew she'd been left by her husband and was now looking for another "M.R.S. degree," as Eliza so cleverly put it–i.e., she was looking to snag another husband to make her a kept woman so she'd never have to put her actual degree to work.

In another life, Walter might have been more susceptible to a woman with a generous laugh and a perky pair, but he'd been tempted by a bigger fish. He let his eyes roam the office to see if *she* was about, but as there was no sight of *her*, he turned his eyes to Eliza.

It was really a shame his oldest and favorite daughter had to degrade herself by working in a place like this, but the department was being so unreasonable. They'd threatened to cut Eliza's funding just because she was taking seven years to complete her graduate degree, with no end to her dissertation in sight. Brilliant minds couldn't just be turned on like a lightswitch, ready on demand. But, as part of her stipulation for maintaining her funding, she now had to work part-time at the front desk of the department offices. And if anyone could pull it off with style and aplomb, it was Eliza.

She grinned conspiratorially at her father before turning her gaze back to her screen. In the reflection of the lenses of her non-prescription glasses, he could see she was on Instagram. "You do remember that you have another daughter on campus who's a student worker?" she reminded him drolly.

"Yes, and I stand by what I said. My favorites are in this room!"

The three of them laughed together. He knew that Penelope had likely been filled in by Eliza with Ana's latest schemes to ruin all their fun, suggesting they go to Gulf Shores for their spring break instead of Ibiza. As if.

It was remarkably easy to fall into this familiar rhythm of snark, pretending as if nothing was amiss. Then again, Walter had spent several weeks already training himself not to jump every time the hit-and-run accident came up, which was far too often, in his opinion, for a scholarship student. Almost easy, too, to forget he was being blackmailed. If that's what was even happening. Perhaps he'd misunderstood the email, and it was merely a friendly warning that he needed to tie up some loose ends.

What is due to myself. Hmm. No. That sounded ominous, and not remotely friendly.

"Tea," he said abruptly to pull himself out of that dark spiral. "A nice afternoon high tea, I think. Who's peckish? I'm buying."

Eliza rolled her eyes theatrically, and Penelope gave a long drawn-out sigh. "Alas, we've both been reprimanded for leaving our posts too often."

Walter frowned at that. Preposterous! He'd only convinced them to take long lunches once, maybe twice a week. There had been that one Friday they'd shut down the office early to take an impromptu drive to New Orleans, but it had been a necessary trip, since there'd been a rumor Taylor Swift was in town. (She hadn't been, but the three of them had enjoyed a wonderful time wandering the French Quarter looking for her.) Considering how many days Penelepe and

Eliza had to actually *be* here, sitting at this dreadful desk, it hardly seemed fair to begrudge them missing a few days here and there.

How important could it be to have someone sitting in the office, anyhow? Eliza and Penelope could answer their emails just as easily from a restaurant as from here.

At the reminder of emails, and how easily they followed one around from place to place, Walter shuddered. If only he could have gotten a good old-fashioned blackmail letter in the mail. He could lock that up in his office and leave it out of sight. But an email...that lurked forever on his laptop, on his phone, his Smart Watch, anywhere he could be reached, just one ping away from ruining everything he'd built all these years.

All at once, it seemed desperately important to Walter that he not be alone. Otherwise he knew he would spiral, and aside from being very bad for his mental health, he imagined it wouldn't do wonders for his skin, either. "Just one of you, then? I'm sure Pen wouldn't mind covering for you, Liza."

Penelope *did* rather look like she minded, though, and Eliza was already shaking her head. "Can't. They've been dropping in to check on us all week, haven't they, Pen? Anyway, there's a cybersale I'm tracking, so I'm better off staying put."

Walter worried he might really need to do something desperate to distract himself, like reach out to Ana to see if she was free to keep him company, when a voice from the hallway caught his attention. "Did I hear someone mention tea?"

For a moment, all thought of blackmailing emails–and anything else for that matter–fled Walter's mind. He turned as if in slow motion to see *her*–the goddess of the Rumford Building, Susan Vernon. Her husband had been the dean of the School of Science and Engineering before his untimely passing. Actually, it had been rather timely for him, seeing as how he was in his late eighties, though his widow was still a woman in her prime–her 40s, if rumor was to be believed, though she didn't look a day over 30. Walter thought this without judgment, since he, too, spent an exorbitant amount of money maintaining a youthful glow and a fashionable exterior, so he understood why it was also rumored that Susan had needed to take on a job in the department office after her husband's passing.

Susan claimed she merely wanted to keep busy, and indeed she was so efficient at organizing everybody and keeping them in line that she'd been nicknamed "Lady Susan" around the office. In truth, this nickname was likely less flattering than Walter imagined it to be, but in his mind there was no better distinction for such a remarkable woman. She *was* a lady, through and through, from the way she carried herself to the way she spoke to the way she smelled–like Portrait of a Lady, if his nostrils didn't fail him, and they rarely did!

"Susan," Walter breathed. "What a lovely surprise."

Susan offered him a radiant smile in return. She was wearing that dark red lipstick he liked so much, that made her look like Rita Hayworth, although it also made it very difficult to keep his eyes from being drawn back to her lips, again and again. She came close to kiss him on the cheek, and he took the opportunity to inhale her. Just the slightest hint of Turkish rose and sandalwood. Exquisite.

"And a treat for me," she told him as she pulled back. "What brings you into our humble corner of the world?"

"Tea." Walter stammered out the word just a bit too quickly. He always found himself acting vaguely like a blushing schoolboy when he was around this woman, not the erudite man of the world he knew himself to be. Forcing himself to take in a deep breath, he counted to three before continuing, "I'd hoped to persuade one of these lovely ladies to join me, but alas, they're unable to break away. I don't suppose...?"

"Tea sounds lovely!" Susan hesitated, worrying her lip. "Though, I wouldn't want Eliza and Penelope to feel burdened by picking up any of my work in my absence."

"They won't mind!" Walter assured her eagerly, though a quick glance at the two women in question made him do a double take. They were both glowering at Susan, although that was simply preposterous. He'd offered them both the chance to go, and they hadn't taken it, so there was no need to be sourpusses about it. He supposed extraordinarily beautiful women always gathered their fair share of critics, though.

He was quickly drawn back into Susan's orbit, by her bright eyes and that lovely red mouth as it broadened into a grin. "Let me just fetch my coat!"

Susan was such a wonderful distraction that for nearly an hour and a half, Walter forgot all his earlier troubles of the day. It wasn't until he excused himself to use the men's room, when he received another ping on his phone, that he felt his stomach lurch with dread. Sure enough, there was another message waiting for him.

$100,000.

Walter gaped at the sum. Who did this person think he was, exactly? He could hardly scrape up $1000, much less a hundred times over. He gazed intently into the mirror, sincerely anxious, but also reveling a bit in how cinematic the moment felt–dramatically searching out his own reflection for answers. The novelty passed quickly, though, as a fresh anxiety spiked through him. Who the devil was this person, and how on earth was he meant to keep them silent when he'd never be able to afford that kind of sum?

He thought he'd done a good enough job composing himself before he returned to the table, but Susan took one look at him and gasped theatrically. "Walter, what is it? Forgive me for saying so, but you look terrible."

This woman could see through him so clearly. Walter squeezed her hand in admiration, doing his best to smile as he retook his seat. "It's nothing. Really. I wouldn't want to spoil our delicious clotted cream."

Susan clasped his fingers with her own. "The cream can wait, Walter. I'm worried about you. You've seemed apprehensive all afternoon."

Had he? Walter thought he'd done a good enough job keeping up with their chatter—all the usual subjects, like which faculty members were letting themselves go, and what they thought of that one exhibit at New York fashion week, and how much they both adored Gwenyth—but Susan had seen through him. He squeezed her hand back. "Sweet Susan. You always think more for others than you do for yourself."

"Not for all others," Susan assured him. "Only those I care *most* about."

Walter gave a shaky laugh. "I wouldn't want to burden you…" He trailed off, though, because the sentiment wasn't entirely true. He *did* want to burden somebody else with this, someone competent and efficient, who would solve all his problems for him.

"None of that, Walter," Susan returned with faux sternness. "Now. Tell me everything. I'm all ears."

So Walter did as he was told, and revealed everything—not just about the emails, but about that night at the Croft Gala, the last cocktail that had pushed him over the edge, the foolhardy decision to drive. "Nothing would have ever come of it if that foolish girl hadn't been out walking on the side of the road," he concluded glumly.

"It was extremely selfish of her," Susan agreed. "She ought to be apologizing to you, really!"

Walter warmed to the idea for a moment before sighing. "It's all about the optics though. That's what President de Bourgh always says. Diversity and inclusivity and student wellness."

Susan shook her head sympathetically. "We truly have fallen from the golden age of education. Professors used to be treated with respect and deference, and now you're basically customer service agents, there to cater to your students' every whim and fancy."

"Terrible. Just terrible." Walter sighed. "But what can I do? If I lose this position…"

Susan sipped at her tea, eying him over the rim of her cup. "You have family money, though, don't you?"

Walter waved a hand dismissively. "Of course, yes...there's the house, and the yacht, the apartment in Miami..." No need to mention that the house was on its second mortgage, the yacht had been reclaimed two summers ago, and the apartment in Miami technically belonged to his cousin. "...but $100,000 is still a steep sum, by any stretch of the imagination. I don't think I can manage that!"

He *knew* he couldn't manage that, but he didn't want to say that to Susan–especially not when she was looking at him with such big, caring eyes, her red lips pursed into a sympathetic pout.

"Of course you can't, not a man accustomed to your lifestyle. And you shouldn't have to, either." Susan squeezed his arm before sitting back, seeming to lose herself in thought for a moment. "You know, a few years back, I had something similar happen to me. Not blackmail, mind you, but I had a man who was following me around. Writing me love letters, breaking into the house to leave me gifts, things like that. I hired a private detective, a very reliable fellow named Manwaring, and he took care of everything for me. Everything! I never heard from the stalker again, and I was able to go on with life as usual."

Walter's heart leaped at the idea. His was a privileged life, but he hadn't realized just how privileged until its absence had been dangled in front of him. "Do you think Manwaring could manage something like this?"

"Oh, absolutely." Susan took another sip of her tea, nodding fervently. "I imagine this would be right in his wheelhouse."

A sudden thought struck Walter, and he frowned. "But that would mean...I'd have to tell him everything, wouldn't I?"

Susan touched his arm again, offering another gentle squeeze. "I trust Manwaring implicitly. He would never betray a confidence." She leaned forward a little to clasp his hand, and her blouse fell open ever so slightly, so he could see the shadow of her breasts. "Please, Walter. You've been so kind, so welcoming to me, when I know others in the department were probably gossiping behind my back. No–don't try to deny it. You've always been my champion. Let me ease some of your burden, Walter. Please. It's what's due to yourself."

Susan's captivating eyes bored into his, hypnotizing him, making him lose himself for a moment. There was something so intoxicating, almost *predatory*, about that red of her mouth...

He blinked. "What did you say?"

"I said you owe it to yourself, Walter," Susan returned smoothly. "Let me return the favor, please."

He released a shaky breath, nodding as he clasped her hands with his. "How can I refuse an entreaty like that?"

Beaming, Susan leaned back again. "You'll see, Walter. You're in excellent hands now. I'll take care of everything. Trust me."

And he did. Walter felt such enormous relief, giving himself over to Susan Vernon. Beyond being simply beautiful, she was the most capable, the most cunning woman he knew. If there was anyone who could get him out of this mess, it was her.

And if there was anything Walter prided himself on, it was being a most excellent judge of character.

"Do we really have to record the conversation?" Walter asked, shifting uncomfortably at the sight of the recorder sitting out on the table between them.

He didn't like this–not one bit. He'd expected Manwaring to be "a man of the people," so to speak, since he was a private detective, and all. The man had certainly physically lived up to his expectations–he had the sort of unshowered, stubbled appeal of a rock musician, but absolutely nothing elegant or refined about him. He'd insisted on conducting this interview in his apartment, which was the sort of basic, Spartan dwelling that always put Walter on edge. No art on the walls. No cashmere blankets or throw pillows to soften the harsh, boxy sofa. He wouldn't be surprised to open the cabinets and find paper plates, for goodness sake!

There was probably a kind of woman who liked Manwaring's brutish appeal, but not Susan, Walter reassured himself. Susan was the picture of elegance, in her ivory wrap dress. She'd probably have grease marks on her when she stood up from the chair, if Manwaring only cleaned as often as he shaved.

As if she sensed his unease, Susan clasped Walter's wrist, giving it a reassuring squeeze. "Manwaring did the same thing when he took on my case. He likes to have a record so he can double-check his facts, even if he's investigating late at night or early in the morning–isn't that right, Manwaring?"

Sitting across the table from them, Manwaring grunted. "Right."

Just like an ape, Walter thought with distaste. He might as well beat his chest with his fists and call himself Tarzan, for all of his verbal capacity and wit.

Manwaring looked to Susan, and a wordless exchange seemed to take place. "Anyone wanna beer?" Without waiting for the response, Manwaring stood and went into the small galley kitchen, not far, but separated from them by a wall.

Now that they were alone once more, Walter searched Susan's flawless face worriedly. "Yes, my dear, but you see, when *you* were interviewed, you were disclosing someone else's crime, not your own."

The corner of Susan's bright red mouth twisted up in a sympathetic smile. "I understand your reservations, Walter. Really, I do." She leaned forward, lowering her voice to a whisper. Their faces were so close now, all Walter would need to do was inch forward, and they'd be kissing. That lush mouth tugged into something playful. "But between you and me, Manwaring doesn't strike me as the sort of criminal mastermind to realize just how this information might be used against you."

She was leaning in so close to him, and looking up at him in a way that felt like a secret. A promise. When he'd arrived at Manwaring's apartment earlier, Susan had been waiting for him at the door, and she'd welcomed him with an embrace, pressing her body fully against his. The potency of that moment came flooding back to him now, her soft exquisiteness and the smell of sandalwood engulfing him.

It took him a moment to realize she was speaking again. "...do you trust me, Walter?" She trailed the pads of her fingers over his wrist, back and forth, back and forth.

"Y-yes." Walter's voice cracked like an aging-out choirboy's. He cleared his throat and tried again. "Yes."

Manwaring returned with three beers, which no one deigned to touch, except for him. Walter was a bit parched, but he wished Manwaring had offered a nice iced tea or flavored lemonade. "When you're ready."

He had a bit of an Australian accent, Walter noticed for the first time, and felt his dislike increase. How distasteful. Australians were such...uncouth personalities.

Susan shifted, so her side was pressed against Walter's—a show of comfort, he was sure, though it *was* rather distracting. He cleared his throat again. "Yes, well. I suppose it began the night of the Croft Gala..."

He proceeded to describe the entire lurid event, as Susan squeezed his thigh sympathetically and Manwaring sipped his beer, watching him expressionlessly.

"...I could see she was hurt, but not mortally wounded. I was panicked, you know, so I didn't really mean to, but I drove away. By the time I realized what I'd done, I thought it would look worse if I went back, so I just went home."

"How did you know she wasn't mortally wounded?" Manwaring asked. "Are you a doctor?"

There was no judgment in his tone, but still, Walter bristled. "Actually, yes, I am a doctor!"

Manwaring said nothing, just watched him.

Walter shifted. "Not a medical doctor, per se, but...she was scratched up. Not bleeding buckets or mangled or anything. Unconscious, but I could see she was still breathing."

"You managed to assess all that, but you were too panicked to stay in place until the police came?"

"Who's side are you on, anyway?" Walter exploded, but Manwaring only smirked at him.

Susan clucked her tongue. "Manwaring, you're being dreadfully unkind." She stroked Walter's back, making soothing noises until Walter felt his blood pressure begin to lower again. Better than yoga, this woman—and that was not a commendation he gave out lightly! "That must have been terribly difficult for you to tell that story, Walter."

"It was." He sulked a little, not so much because he was still upset, but because he loved her coddling attention, and wanted to bask in it for as long as he could.

Her soft, soothing fingers danced up and down his spine. "What did you do with the car afterward?"

It felt so good, Walter almost purred. "I hid it in the garage for a few weeks. Told Ana I'd decided to take up biking to save some money."

"That was very clever of you, Walter. Is it still in the garage now?"

"I sold it." More accurately, Walter had strong-armed one of his undergrads into helping him figure out one of those online sites, where you could sell cars quick for cash, no questions asked.

"Hmm. That makes sense. I suppose we don't need it, though, do we? We have enough here."

There was nothing different in Susan's tone; it was still the same soft, cajoling voice she'd been using with him, but there was something so...*direct* in it. Walter blinked in confusion, taking a moment to catch up to what it was that Susan was saying. "Have enough for what?"

But he realized, looking up, that Susan hadn't been talking to him. She was looking at Manwaring now, and the two of them were smiling at each other in a familiar and *knowing* sort of way that made Walter instinctively bristle. Still stroking his back with one hand,

Susan reached with the other to take Manwaring's offered beer. She put it to her blood red lips and took a long, deep sip.

"So, Walter," she said when she was finished. "About that $100,000. We prefer cryptocurrency. We can take smaller payments, of course, if that's amenable to you, but there will be interest incurred if it isn't paid off in a timely manner."

Walter gaped at her, then at Manwaring, then back at her again. "This was… you mean *you*…?"

"Yes, darling." Susan took another sip of the beer. "Now you may have been foolish, but please don't be stupid. Let's catch up quickly and not ask a lot of inane questions, please."

It was precisely the right thing to say to Walter. He wanted to sputter. He wanted to shout! But he did not want to look insipid. That would be too embarrassing. "How could you have known?" he decided on finally. That wasn't too inane of a question, was it?

"The student who you asked to help you sell the car came in to complain at the department office," Susan informed him. "He said you threatened to fail him. Tsk-tsk, Walter. That wasn't a very appropriate use of power, was it? Luckily for you, I smoothed things over quickly. Luckily for me, Eliza and Penelope had left early that day because of a pedicure emergency, so I was the only one in the office. After that, it was a simple matter of deduction. Why would you need to sell a car so desperately, so soon after a mysterious hit and run just off-campus that had never been solved?"

"It could have been a coincidence," Walter protested.

"It could have, but it wasn't." Susan smiled at him, and even now, Walter had to marvel at how beautiful she was, how flawlessly lovely. "I have remarkably good instincts–don't I, Manwaring?"

Manwaring was grinning like a dirty, handsome jack o'lantern across the table at Walter. "The best."

"And how does *he* come into play?" Walter refused to speak to the man directly, now that he knew he was nothing but a lackey. "You wanted some muscle onboard, in case I turned against you?"

Susan laughed aloud at that. "Oh, Walter." She sounded

genuinely fond of him, and she reached up to brush one of his well-coiffed curls out of his eyes.

It was possible, he thought, that she really did like him. Perhaps she was desperate for money. The sudden death of her husband must have left her in a bad spot. And it wasn't dignified, really, for a woman of her stature to be working in a lowly department office. Perhaps, if he could just explain to her that he would help her in some other way, that they didn't have to go this route...

Something caught his attention out of the corner of his eye. It was a flash of red, something Manwaring was holding in his hands. Walter realized with a sudden jolt of comprehension that it was Susan's bare foot, in Manwaring's lap, and that he was leisurely massaging its arch as the two of them conversed.

Susan and *Manwaring*? Now Walter really did feel the fool. To be blackmailed for a career-ending crime was one thing. To lose a woman to a *private detective* was quite another. And an Australian, at that! Good God, was there no decency in the world?

"How could you have used me this way?" Walter snapped at Susan, not ready yet to admit to his own dashed hopes, and instead fixating his anger on something easier to grasp. "I thought we were friends."

"We are, darling!" Susan looked genuinely hurt at the accusation. "Haven't we always had such fun together? I care about you. That's why I'd rather it come from me, than someone else. People can really be so cruel."

Across the table, Manwaring laughed under his breath, and Walter had to suppress a shudder. Yes, he could imagine all too well that this man could be cruel. That was why Susan needed him, he suspected. A little brute strength to add some real threat to her schemes.

"What do you say, Walter?" Susan said, drawing his attention back to her lovely face. "Can you make the payment all at once, or would you like to go on a plan? Manwaring is very good at keeping people on schedule, aren't you, Manwaring?"

Walter blinked at her in astonishment. "I don't have $100,000. Are you insane? I'm a professor at a private institution. A *teaching* institution, at that! I'm so poor my youngest daughter will only let me go to Starbucks once a week."

"Cash poor, maybe," Susan agreed. "But what about the house, the yacht, the apartment in Miami?"

Walter laughed aloud at that. "I was lying, of course, to impress you. The house is on its second mortgage. The yacht– gone! The apartment was sold off a long time ago. There are no assets. I couldn't scrape up $1,000 to pay you, much less $100,000!" He was laughing so hard now he was crying, and he pulled his embroidered silk handkerchief from his blazer pocket to wipe at his eyes. "You picked the wrong target for blackmail, I'm afraid."

His laughter rang throughout the now-quiet room—-too quiet, Walter realized suddenly. Much too quiet. When he finished wiping his eyes, he saw Manwaring and Susan were no longer smiling, but staring at each other intently. All at once, Susan looked years older to him, nothing soft or sweet about her.

She turned to look back at him again, leveling him with her cool gaze. "That's very disappointing to hear, Walter. That would have made it much easier for you, if you had the cash or assets on-hand. But I'm sure you'll find a way to come up with the money, one way or another."

Walter shook his head. "I really can't–"

"You *really* can." Susan's voice was sweet again, but cool as ice now. "Or I'd hate to think what might happen to your daughters. Your job. Your reputation."

It would be gone, Walter realized–all of it. It was worse than simply the threat of imprisonment. It was the loss of freedom, real freedom. Cool iced drinks from his favorite trendy coffee shop, online shopping for the newest business casual shorts and boat shoes. Gossiping with his stylist every other week, overtipping his manicurist to show he could afford it, even when he couldn't. Being

Professor Walter Elías, respected and admired, a fixture in his small campus town.

And all of it could be gone, gone, in the blink of an eye.

As if she sensed his understanding, Susan smiled, and leaned in to kiss his cheek. "I believe in you, Walter. I know you'll find a way."

Or else, went the word unspoken, in Manwaring's grim set of his jaw across the table.

Or else, it was silently agreed, on Susan's smiling, blood-red lips.

The End

Read more about "Lady" Susan, Manwaring, Walter, and more in the Austen University Mysteries series - Book 3 will be coming out in 2025! Catch up on Book 1 and Book 2, and the two prequel novellas, through the Amazon link below!

Elizabeth Gilliland is the author of the Austen University

Mysteries series, including What Happened on Box Hill, The Portraits of Pemberley, and two prequel novellas, Dear Prudent Elinor and Sly Jane Fairfax. (Look out for book three sometime next year!) She has written and presented at various academic conferences on Jane Austen and wrote her dissertation on Jane Austen adaptations, dedicating herself to watch the lake dive scene as many times as necessary for scholarly pursuit. She also writes Gothic horror as E. Gilliland and romance as Lissa Sharpe, and she is the co-founder of Bayou Wolf Press.

Website: www.bayouwolfpress.com

Twitter: https://twitter.com/egilliland

Facebook: https://www.facebook.com/profile.php?id=100094046020056

Goodreads: https://www.goodreads.com/author/show/21986541.Elizabeth_Gilliland

Blog: https://lissag7.medium.com/

Newsletter: Signup form at https://www.bayouwolfpress.com/

Amazon: https://www.amazon.com/stores/author/B09LHV8VKV?ingress=0&visitId=00a42e2f-c711-4615-a050-9d2250f9f124&ref_=sr_ntt_srch_lnk_1

ABOUT THE PUBLISHER

Bayou Wolf Press is an independent publisher of quality fiction. If you enjoyed this book and would like to support us, the best thing you can do is leave a review on Amazon, Goodreads, or wherever you review books. If you'd like to learn more about our press, sign up for our newsletter, and stay informed on upcoming books, please visit www.bayouwolf.com